Professional letter writer Holly Chamberlain and Reverend Grayson Clark love each other, but shyness seals their lips. Will help from the Christmas Spirit and an over the top production of *A Christmas Carol* lead them to meet under the mistletoe for the first of a lifetime of kisses?

Grayson held out his gloved hand, and she accepted it, feeling a surprising strength in his palm and fingers, and the earlier warmth became a flow of heat surging through her. Standing beneath the swirling snow, Holly would not have moved for the world.

A Christmas Proposal

To keep away the fortune-hunters, heiress Cassandra Barnwell makes a deal with confirmed bachelor Lord Brandon Russell. Pretend to court her during the Christmas season, and she'll back his archeology expeditions. But with the holiday upon them, and their attraction growing stronger with every meeting, which will they choose? Go their separate ways or ring in the New Year as husband and wife?

The world disappeared at the taste of Brandon's lips, sweet and soft, and the sound of her heart all but drowned out the cheering of the children. His arms about her were warm and strong, and Cassandra knew if they were trapped forever beneath the dome of a snow globe, she would be forever happy.

The Comet that Came for Christmas

Years ago, star crossed lovers Victoria Hawthorne and Jake Dillon lost their chance for happily ever after. Will an unexpected meeting at Christmas-and a little help from Haley's comet-bring them together again?

Her fingers wrapped around Jake's palm, and as she descended the steps, he impulsively slid his hands around her waist and lowered her to the ground. Victoria's hands reached up to his shoulders and her eyes widened, watching him and waiting.

"You forgot to wear your hat," she whispered, brushing snowflakes from his hair. "You don't want to get sick, do you?"

"No." Jake's heart began to hammer with a rib-bruising force and he lowered his head to brush his lips against hers in a feathering sweep.

Happy Holidays!

Karen Hall

Love Came For Christmas

Karen Hall

DEDICATION
This book is dedicated to my friend Leanne Tyler who always fixes all my computer glitches – You Go Girl!

OTHER STORIES BY
Karen Hall

A Christmas Proposal

Christmas Stockings

Star Carol for Celeste

The Comet That Came For Christmas

You're My Secret Santa, Baby

Christmas Stockings

Chapter One-🪶

London. December 1892

"Your skin, I would cover with endless kisses and—"

"Mr. Smithson!" Holly Chamberlain snatched off her glasses—used only for reading of course—and gave the gentleman across the desk a stern frown. "You cannot say that to a lady you hope to make your bride. At least not yet."

Mr. Smithson blushed to the roots of his fair hair. "I beg your pardon, Miss Chamberlain. But when I think of Penelope, I am so overcome with emotion I can hardly control myself."

"Of course." Holly agreed, settling the glasses back on her nose. "But you don't want to scare her away with your boldness, do you?"

"Heaven forbid!" Mr. Smithson vowed fervently, raising his hands in supplication. "What do you suggest?"

Holly tapped her chin. "Why not say, 'your luminous skin outshines all other pearls'?"

Mr. Smithson's eyes grew misty. "Oh, Miss Chamberlain. How fortunate are we bachelors, clumsy with words, to have you. You help us convey our thoughts and deepest emotions for our beloved ladies."

Holly bit the inside of her cheek to hide her smile at his lengthy praise. "You're very welcome, Mr. Smithson. Writing letters, especially love letters, is a small talent, but I am happy to use it to help others. Now, let us go on."

By the hour's end, Holly had finished with her suggestions, and given a copy of the letter to Mr. Smithson to re-write in his own hand. The smiling gentleman handed over the required fee and departed, whistling a Gilbert and Sullivan tune. Holly had no doubt that by Advent's completion, she would be reading the announcement of his engagement to one Penelope Witherspoon, insuring Holly's success as the best letter writer in London. She could write a love letter for almost anyone to anyone.

Except herself.

Because no young lady of her social standing would dare to write a love letter to the man of her dreams. A man who existed in the form of one Grayson Clark, scholar and rector of St. Martin in the Pines. A man who was perfection itself.

Not that Holly didn't have her admirers. She had several, and to be sure, they were all handsome and accomplished and successful. A woman would be pleased by the attentions of even one of them. Theodore-Theo to his friends-Barrett in particular had been most ardent in his attentions. The barrister's considerable charm had made him very popular in Holly's social circle, and more than one young lady had given Holly the evil eye as it became more and more evident that Theo was launching a campaign to win Holly's affections. A campaign encouraged by Holly's father, Phineas

"You couldn't do better," Papa had wheedled only last night. "Theo is bound to receive a knighthood by the time he's forty. He's brilliant."

And as full of himself as a Spotted Dick pudding. Holly thought, massaging her hands. Her subtle attempts at discouraging Theo's attentions had only been met by increased fervor and no doubt prompted by Holly's generous dowry. Theo was quite well off in his own right, and wouldn't need Holly's money, but sometimes being the only child of a successful businessman who owned London's largest chain of tobacco and candy shops had its drawbacks.

Holly turned her gaze to the window. The overcast late Friday afternoon sky suggested snow was on the way. Snow at Christmas. How perfectly, wonderfully romantic. Her mind drifted to scenes from her favorite book of love stories. Carriage rides over snow-covered fields, perhaps in search of the perfect Christmas tree. Long walks at twilight with silvery flakes floating down from the heavens, while holding the arm of someone most dear. A stolen kiss under the mistletoe—

The bell over the front door jingled in greeting, snatching her from her reverie. Holly quickly smoothed her hair and set her features into a welcoming smile. In the outer chamber she heard the birdlike chirp of her assistant, Celeste Stillwell, followed by the rustle of her skirts as she burst into Holly's office and closed the door behind her.

"Holly," she called, her china blue eyes wide. "You're simply not going to believe who is here!"

"The Prince of Wales?" Holly joked. Celeste always grew excited by just about any visitor.

"No, it's Grayson Clark!" Only Celeste knew of Holly's true feelings for the clergyman, and if possible, her eyes grew even wider.

Holly's fingers curled around the arms of her chair and a rod of newly poured steel replaced her spine. "What does he want?" she whispered.

"H-he said something about hiring you to write a letter." Celeste darted a glance over her shoulder as if the man himself stood behind her, before returning her gaze to meet Holly's. "What should I tell him?"

Commanding her heart to stop its furious gallop, Holly said, "Show him in."

Nodding, Celeste opend the door and scampered into the hall, only to return seconds later. "Mr. Grayson Clark," she intoned solemnly, stepping into the room.

After a quick glance in the wall mirror, Holly snatched off her glasses, and put them on the desk before standing. She folded her trembling hands and waited.

The tall, thin figure who followed Celeste wore clerical black, with a white band around the collar of his neatly pressed shirt. A wave of auburn hair swept back from his handsome features, and his amber eyes glittered at the women. Holly just barely contained her sigh of appreciation. No wonder half the women in the parish-young and old-showered him with invitations to tea and dinner on the unlikely pretext of fattening him up.

And no doubt looking him over as a prospective matrimonial candidate. Holly had heard rumors that no less than Miss Priscilla Honeywell, granddaughter of Sir Cyrus Honeywell, baronet, amateur scholar and chief patron of the Queen's Players, a local dramatic society, had her eye on Mr. Grayson Clark. Even Holly's own kitchen maid, Clara, who was cast as Martha Cratchit in the Queen's Players' upcoming production of *A Christmas Carol,* said Miss Honeywell, cast as the Ghost of Christmas Present, did everything but openly flirt with Grayson Clark. Harold, the Chamberlain's coachman, cast as Fizziwig in the same play, also had commented on Miss Honeywell's attentions to Mr. Clark.

His smile sent a flush of warmth hurtling over Holly's skin. "Good afternoon, Miss Chamberlain," he said. "I hope I find you well?"

"Very well, Mr. Clark," she said, proud her voice did not tremble. "You remember my friend, Miss Celeste Stillwell?"

"Yes indeed," he returned, giving Celeste the same smile. "She greeted me most kindly."

If it were not for Celeste's death grip on the doorknob, she surely would have slid to the floor beneath the force of that smile. But like Holly, she managed not to croak out her words. "Thank you, Mr. Clark. Holly, I'll be right outside if you should need me."

She stepped into the outer office again, pulling the door not quite shut behind her. Holly gestured at the wooden captain's chair before her desk. "Please be seated, Mr. Clark."

He waited until she sat before lowering his long body into the indicated spot and placing the folder he carried on the corner of her desk. "Are you looking forward to the upcoming Christmas season, Miss Chamberlain?"

"I love Christmas," Holly told him. "It's my favorite time of year. And you surely must be busy learning your role of Bob Crachit for the Queen's Players in their production of *A Christmas Carol* at St. Martin's?"

His expression turned solemn. "Yes, and it's because of that production I come to you today. The Queen's Players and St. Martin's needs your help."

"I thought you told Celeste you needed help with a letter of some kind?" Holly could hardly believe that an Oxford scholar needed help with writing anything.

"There is that," he said. "But our Mrs. Crachit has broken her ankle and we are in desperate need of a replacement. Matthew Timmons, our director has seen you in other productions and asked me to be his emissary to come and beg you to please join our little cast."

Holly blinked. "Me?"

"Yes indeed," Mr. Clark affirmed with a quick nod. "Matthew said your performance in last year's Christmas Pantomime at St. Bart's was excellent."

"Well–" Holly hesitated. Theo was playing Scrooge in the St. Martin's production, and even with such a small role as Mrs. Crachit, rehearsals would put her constantly in his company. As it would with the man seated across from her. Holly's heart skipped a beat at the thought.

"Well," she repeated, "I suppose I could do that."

"Excellent!" Mr. Clark declared, opening the folder and taking out a large sheaf of papers. "Here are your scenes. We have a rehearsal tomorrow afternoon at two o'clock and Sunday afternoon as well. I know that St. Martin in the Pines is not the most elegant church in the parish, but it does boast a very large stage in the Parish Hall, with plenty of room behind it for actors to wait and props to be stored and—"

"And where you are the rector," Holly said as she took the papers. Her fingertips grazed his, sending a jolt of warmth up her arm.

"Well, yes," he said, a note of mock solemnity entering his voice. "There is that."

They shared a laugh. He had a nice laugh, not too loud, and one that brought a light to his eyes. Miss Jane Austen should have mentioned that men too could have "very fine eyes."

"So." Holly picked up her pen. "As to the letter Celeste mentioned you needed?"

His cheerful expression changed to one of such solemnity that Holly nearly gasped aloud as she watched the light fade from his eyes. "Ah, yes," he said after a long moment. "That is to say——"

If she were not sure of his confidence in all matters, Holly would swear he was nervous. "Do go on," she urged.

"It is a matter of the utmost delicacy," he began. "I rely on your total discretion."

"You have it," Holly said. "I could not have developed my clientele otherwise. And I do but help people frame their thoughts. Their words are their own, with some help."

"I have a friend who desires to make his affection known to a lady of his acquaintance," Mr. Clarkson said slowly. "He is a rather shy fellow, and his handwriting at best is –is–"

"Illegible?" Holly prompted.

"More like hieroglyphics," he corrected ruefully. "Deciphering his correspondence is a near impossible task. He is rather good with words but needs a scribe to write them down on paper. I understand you often write letters for those who have not the knowledge or the skill?"

"I do help those who need to have letters written or read, sometimes to family and sometimes ones of business. And if I can help in matters of the heart, so much the better."

He regarded her thoughtfully, as if considering her words. "And your father does not object to your working?"

"Papa has always remembered how his own grandfather could not read or write," Holly said wistfully. "And yet it did not stop him from opening the first tobacco and candy shops that carry our name to this day."

"Who in London does not know of Chamberlain's Sweets and Tobacco?" Mr. Clarkson struck a pose. "'A smoke for every taste and a sweet for every tooth.' "

Holly laughed as he quoted the Chamberlain's slogan. "Papa agreed with my desire to honor great-grandfather's memory by offering the help to others that he did not have."

"You have a generous heart, Miss Chamberlain," Mr. Clark said gently. "Not many young ladies would do what you do."

"Well, since my sewing and knitting skills are non-existent, I can hardly make garments for the poor." Holly pulled an expression of mock resignation. "Now, back to the business at hand. Why does your friend not simply come and ask me himself to write the letters?"

"As I have said, he is a shy man who prefers to keep his personal affairs as private as possible. And so he has engaged me to acquire your services. I would write them myself, but my own handwriting is at times poor, and my friend desires the script to be as beautiful as the receiver of the letter."

And because I haven't the guts to tell you myself that I love and adore you above all women. I only hope I can screw up the courage to give you the letters. Grayson tried hard not to stare at the brunette beauty who haunted his every waking moment and nearly as much as his sleeping ones. A lone drop of perspiration crept down his neck and then his back. Thank goodness his wardrobe was full of freshly laundered shirts and collars.

She lowered her gaze and seemed to be studying the desk's polished surface from beneath her long lashes. Then she looked up, and her chocolate-colored eyes twinkled at him.

"You're his Miles Standish, aren't you? Or perhaps his Cyrano de Bergerac?" She cocked her head in study of him and added, "But without the nose of course."

A laugh escaped him and he said, "No, thank goodness for that."

She joined his laughter, hers a light, sparkling sound and a tiny ray of hope sparked in his heart. Perhaps there might be a chance for him after all.

"Well," the object of his dreams said, pulling a single sheet of paper towards her from the stack on the edge of her desk. "Shall we begin?"

Grayson cleared his throat. "Very well." He reached into an inner coat pocket, took out a folded sheet of paper and held it up. "I took the liberty of having him dictate his letter to me."

"A wise idea," Miss Chamberlain affirmed with a nod.

"Perhaps I should read it aloud first, so you will understand the flow of his language?"

She nodded again and Grayson unfolded the sheet, staring hard at the penmanship that had been the despair of his instructors at Oxford. "Since the moment of our first meeting, you have stirred my heart," he read aloud. "Such beauty, grace and gentleness combined is a rare treasure, one I could hardly dream of one day having as my own. No man could deserve such a treasure, but men will dream, and often of that which they cannot have. I am such a man. I hope that you may consider me a dear friend, and will one day consider me more. Your devoted servant—" Grayson stopped and looked at Miss Chamberlain. "That's all," he said.

"How very eloquent," she said softly. "The lady your friend wishes to impress will undoubtedly be moved."

"Do you really think so?"

"I have no doubt. Now if you will read it to me again, slowly so I can—"

The door banged opened and Theodore Barrett, stepped into the room, exuding the confidence Grayson so envied. Well-tailored and well-shod, he carried the air of a man who always gets what he wants.

And he, no doubt, like Grayson, very much wanted Miss Holly Chamberlain's attention and affections.

"Good afternoon, Holly," he said. "Your father has sent me 'round to fetch you home to supper." His blue eyes flickered in Grayson's direction. "Hello, Grayson," he greeted. "Fancy meeting you here."

"Theodore." Grayson clipped off the word.

"Mr. Clark is here on a mission for a friend," Miss Chamberlain told him. "You and Papa will have to wait."

Theodore affected a deep sigh. "If I must. Is there any tea to be had?"

"You'll have to ask Celeste," was her reply. "Run along now. Mr. Clark and I have business to finish."

She waved in dismissal, and with another sigh, Theodore withdrew and closed the door behind him.

"Celeste?" they heard him call. "Is there tea? Be a good girl and fetch me a cup."

Grayson noted the slight frown drawing Miss Chamberlain's eyebrows together. "He seems very confident in his expectations of getting what he wants," he said.

She spread her hands. "Theodore is a barrister," she said, as if that explained everything.

"Ah," Grayson said, his heart sinking. How could a mere clergyman, even one with a small private income, compete with a barrister's eloquence? Then he forced a smile and said, "I don't want to keep you from your father. Shall we finish my friend's letter?"

"Most certainly," she said, reaching for a pen. "I believe it began, 'Since the moment of our first meeting…' "

Too soon they had finished, and after allowing enough time for the ink to dry, Miss Chamberlain handed it to Grayson. Her fingertips grazed his, and an unexpected, but not unwelcome heat jolted up his arm.

"There you are, Mr. Clark," she said. "Is that all?"

Grayson's thoughts whirled like mad. "Actually, I believe my friend may want more than one letter. But he wants to know the lady's reaction before he proceeds. Do you require payment now or later?"

Her brown eyes sparkled. "Let's wait until we know what the lady thinks," she suggested. "And how could I not trust such an honest courier?"

The door opened again to show Theodore carrying a large tray with a pot of tea, and two cups.

Two. Grayson might not be a barrister, but he knew when to take a hint. He placed the precious letter in the folder, stood, and inclined his head. "I will convey this letter to my friend with all speed," he said. "Thank you for your help, Miss Chamberlain. Good day to you. I expect I'll see you at rehearsal tomorrow afternoon, Theodore?"

Barrett's dark eyebrows rose as if in surprise at such a question. "Since I'm playing Scrooge, of course you will."

"Have you finished memorizing your lines for Act Two?" A most un-clergy like feeling of smug satisfaction surged through Grayson as he recalled how the barrister had struggled at last week's rehearsal.

"Very nearly," Theodore said loftily. "I'll be ready by tomorrow."

"Good." Grayson stood. "I'll let Miss Chamberlain tell you her news. Give my best regards to your father, Miss Chamberlain."

He left, and a moment later, the bell over the front door jingled in departure. Theo set the tray on Holly's desk and raised his eyebrows. "What news do you have for me?"

"Matthew Timmons sent Mr. Clark to ask me to play Mrs. Crachit in St. Martin's production of *A*

Christmas Carol ," Holly explained, filling their cups with a steaming Darjeeling.

"Why, that's splendid," Theo declared. "And perhaps you can help me finish memorizing my lines after dinner tonight? I can hardly fail with so charming a coach."

"If you like," Holly said. How hard could it be for a man in love with the sound of his own voice to memorize lines for a play?

Chapter Two-🐚

Grayson made his way down the street, hands jammed in his coat pockets, his folder tucked under his arm. The thought of being on stage with Holly Chamberlain should make him the happiest of men.

And few, if any of their scenes, would include the insufferable Theodore Barrett. Grayson wouldn't mind calling up a ghost or two to frighten the barrister right out of London.

The wind picked up and he pulled his coat more tightly about him. In spite of its only being half past four in the afternoon, the electric streetlights already glimmered overhead, casting a golden glow onto the streets below. People hurried by, some carrying bags no doubt filled with early Christmas gifts.

Christmas gifts. Grayson slowed his walk to examine the decorated shop windows. He needed to find gifts for his younger brother and sisters at home in Kent. With his salary—not to mention the recent legacy a distant relative had left each of them—the cost of the purchases was not a problem. It was buying for his notoriously choosy three younger sisters–Rebecca, Marian, and Susannah–that took so much time. At least his brother, Hugh would be happy with a new cricket bat. He turned down Chestnut Street to start his search.

Cobalt and amethyst bolts of silk artfully draped over the shelves in a shop window stopped Grayson's progress. Christmas ornaments shimmered from a decorated tree on a pedestal, and a set of foot-high carved wooden soldiers faced each other, ready for battle. A quick glance at the sign overhead showed this establishment to be Harrell's Fine Gifts. Another blast of cold wind sent Grayson hurrying inside.

"Good afternoon, sir!" A plump, pretty woman with bright blonde hair called from behind the front counter. "Welcome to Harrell's Fine Gifts. How may I serve you today?"

"I'm looking for Christmas gifts for my siblings," Grayson said, returning her smile.

"We carry many lovely items, sir, for all tastes and pocketbooks," the woman told him. "I'm Mrs. Harrell. Is there anything in particular you wanted to find?"

"I'm not sure," Grayson admitted. "This is my first day of shopping."

"Might I suggest a new Christmas stocking to begin, sir?" Mrs. Harrell pointed at a mock mantle from where a long row of stockings hung, each with a large elaborate initial embroidered on the front.

"Those are very nice," Grayson said, walking across the room to examine them. "Do you have them in all letters?"

"Bless you, sir, yes! They're one of our most popular items. I've got girls who work on them almost all year 'round. People start placing orders as early as February, 'specially if they want the one with more detailed work."

"I think that would make a good start." Grayson returned to the counter and took out his wallet. "I need four, with the letters, M, H, R, and S. Ones like you have over there will do just fine."

Mrs. Harrell rang a bell on the counter and a girl came from behind a curtain. Mrs. Harrell gave her Grayson's order and she departed, returning several minutes later with a stack of brightly wrapped flat boxes. She gave them to Mrs. Harrell, smiled at Grayson and disappeared again behind the curtain.

"That will be two pounds, sir," Mrs. Harrell said as she put the boxes into a sack. "That may seem a bit much, but I want to pay the girls well, and it helps pay for the wrapping paper." She winked and said, "No offense, sir, but I've never found a man who could wrap a package well. He might be able to cut up a Christmas goose like a surgeon, but he's all thumbs when it comes to wrapping a present."

"And to that I say, amen!" Grayson paid her, put away his wallet and took the gifts from her. "I wish you a good afternoon."

"Thank you sir. Come again. We're open until ten on Christmas Eve."

Grayson exited the shop, found an omnibus and rode it back to St. Martin's. Mrs.Ramsey, his housekeeper, was waiting in the front hall of the rectory.

"Good afternoon, Mrs. Ramsey." Grayson handed her the folder and sack before shrugging out of his coat, and hanging it along with his hat on the hall tree in the corner. "May I trouble you for a cup of tea? It's brisk outside."

"You have a visitor," she answered, giving him back his things and planting her hands firmly on her broad hips. "It's himself. I've put him in the parlor." Irritation had replaced her usual cherry tone.

Grayson withheld his sigh of impatience. "Tobias Small?"

Her frown was deep enough for both of them. "The same."

Grayson forced his features into a mask of neutrality at the mention of the austere and stern man that was St. Martin's former rector. Despite his retirement three years ago, Tobias Small continued to "drop by" St. Martin's regularly to "check on things." That he was good friends with Cyrus Honeywell, the senior warden, did not make things any easier. Grayson had no doubt the two men got together for a good chinwag more often than half the matrons in St. Martin's choir, and that Grayson was the chief source of their gossip.

"Indeed?" Grayson gave her the bag from Harrell's. "Well, then you'd best bring in tea with all possible speed."

"It's already there." Mrs. Ramsey cocked her head at the door. "Best hurry."

Nodding in silent agreement, Grayson hurried to the parlor. Behind its oak door, a silver-haired man stood before the fireplace, cup already in hand. He stared at Grayson and frowned. "Mr. Clark," he said, the chill in his voice matching the one in his dark eyes.

"Mr. Small," Grayson returned, forcing his legs to travel slowly across the room. *He*, after all, was now rector of St. Martin in the Pines. Grayson stopped to pour a cup of tea and noted with quiet delight that Mrs. Ramsey had not sent in any cakes or scones. He allowed himself a moment to take several sips before asking, "How may I help you?"

The older man barely hid his scowl. "I've come to discuss a matter of some importance with you concerning St. Martin's. May we sit?"

"Certainly." Grayson waited until the older man sat in the room's best chair before choosing the one opposite. "Again, how may I help you?"

"You are no doubt aware that St. Martin's is in need of a new roof." Small's tone suggested that Grayson was somehow responsible for the problem.

"Yes, and we have been trying to raise funds to replace, or at least repair it," Grayson said. "But times are hard for some of our folk. And what with Christmas approaching, they will be wanting to save for their families."

Something resembling a smile threatened to raise the corners of Mr. Small's thin lips. "Well, I think I may know of a solution."

"I'd be delighted if you would share it with me." At least Grayson was not stretching the truth when he said that.

"I have heard from more than one source that Miss Priscilla Honeywell is fond of you," Mr. Small said. "Perhaps I should say *very* fond of you."

Good Heavens! Grayson swallowed the words before he choked on them. "And what does this have to do with St. Martin's roof?"

The almost smile inched a fraction. "Miss Honeywell's grandfather, Sir Cyrus Honeywell has suggested to me that any particular attention to her from you could result in a generous donation to St. Martin's, if you know what I mean."

So it hadn't been Grayson's imagination. The porcelain skinned beauty's dainty but obvious flattery *had* been flirtation! Clearing his throat, Grayson asked, "Are you saying that any attentions I pay to Miss Honeywell might—"

"*Will*, my boy, will." Condescension fairly dripped from Small's voice. "Mr. Honeywell is determined that if it is within his power, he will get his granddaughter whatever she wants. And she is, I believe, in St. Martin's cast of *A Christmas Carol*?"

You know that she is, you old busybody. Grayson nodded.

"Well, there you have it. Just turn on that charm you used to get the Altar Guild to sew new linens for us instead of us having to buy them, and we'll have a new roof by Easter." Small moved his glance from Grayson's face to the tea tray with its lack of food and his frown returned.

"I'll give it serious consideration, sir," Grayson said, hoping his grip on the teacup didn't result in the handle breaking. *About ten seconds worth.*

"See that you do." Small got to his feet, put his cup on a nearby table and crossed the room to open the door. "Mrs. Ramsey?" he called. "My coat and hat if you please."

Grayson waited until the front door clicked to a close before putting his cup aside. "Good Heavens," he said again to the now quiet room. "What am I going to do?"

Chapter Three-🌿

"Places again, everyone, places!" Matthew Timmons shouted. "We've only a few hours to get this right, so let's make the best of it! Ghost of Christmas Present, are you ready?"

"Indeed I am," Priscilla Honeywell nearly purred her answer as she smiled in Grayson Clark's direction. Holly gritted her teeth at the clergyman's returning smile. It was better than throwing a fit. And it was beastly unfair that Priscilla's ghost got to wear a beautiful silver robe while Holly's Mrs. Cratchit wore a plain dress "made brave with ribbons." How could she possibly compete with a silver robe?

"Scrooge?" Matthew shouted. "Where are you?"

"Just coming," Theo answered, appearing out of the wings.

"Cratchit family, take your places! Bob and Tiny Tim, get ready for your entrance," Matthew directed. "We start with Martha's entrance."

The action began and Holly envisioned herself as a married woman with many children, making do on fifteen bob a week. The younger actors recited their lines perfectly and she responded in kind. Off to one side, Theo and Priscilla's characters observed in silence.

The door built into the set swung open and oh my goodness, there was Grayson, costumed as poorly as she, with little Dick Allen perched on his shoulder. The action proceeded with Grayson/Bob's happy surprise at Martha's homecoming and then she and her brothers hustling Tiny Tim off stage.

"And how did our little Tim behave in church?" Holly asked, watching Grayson/Bob Cratchit unwind the required three feet of scarf.

"As good as gold and—"

"Stop!" Matthew shouted. "Something's not right."

"With our lines?" Holly asked, sure that they were.

"No." Matthew came forward and stared at the pair, tapping his chin with his ever present pencil. "Something's not right between the two of you. I know! Grayson, you're going to have to kiss her."

"What?" Holly squeaked.

"What?" Grayson Clark's tenor voice rose an octave.

"Well, on the cheek," Matthew amended. "You are supposed to be married. We want this to be realistic, after all. You don't mind terribly, do you Holly?"

Thank you, thank you, thank you, Matthew! Holly's heart sang, but she kept her lips pressed together in a frown of concentration. "Not at all," she said at last. "As long as Mr. Clark has no objections."

Mr. Clark darted a look at Priscilla. She smiled and fluttered her eyelashes and Holly considered undoing the many ribbons of her own costume and tying up Priscilla with them and leaving her somewhere.

"I suppose not," Mr. Grayson said at last, returning his gaze to Holly's face.

"Excellent." Matthew struck his open palm with a fist. "Let's try it. Cratchits, back on stage. Clara, make your entrance as Martha again, if you please."

Her heart pounding with a rib bruising force, Holly managed to make her way through the scene with her "children" until Grayson entered again with little Dick on his shoulder. Soon enough, the children had departed again, leaving the Cratchits alone.

"And how was our Tim in church this afternoon?" *Lord, I'm changing my lines, but Grayson Clark is about to kiss me!"* Holly stepped forward to help him with the long, long scarf.

And then he was leaning toward her until he was so close Holly could catch the faint scent of something sweet and spicy. His lips gently grazed her right cheek and if he had not laid his hand under her elbow, the light in his eyes would have buckled Holly's knees, sending her right into his arms in front of the entire cast.

"As good as gold and better," Grayson/Bob answered with far more tenderness in his voice than before. "He said he hoped that when the other people in the church saw him, a crippled child, they would remember at Christmas who healed the lame and made the blind to see."

And then incredibly, his voice broke, and his eyes filled with tears. Holly instinctively reached into her dress pocket for a handkerchief, took it out, and gently dabbed the area under his eyes. "Don't cry, my dear," she said softly. "Please don't cry."

He gave her a lopsided smile and then placing his hands on her arms, leaned forward to kiss her on the forehead. If he had not been holding her in place, Holly would have soared right up to the ceiling and through the roof, straight to Heaven.

"Oh, I say, that's brilliant!" Matthew shouted from down in front. "Absolutely brilliant!"

"Can we please get on with it?" Theo called, brushing the front of his Scrooge's ratty dressing gown.

"It is getting rather late," Priscilla agreed, adjusting her silk flowered crown. "And Grandpapa wants Grayson to come to dinner this evening to talk about the new roof for St. Martin's."

"Right you are," Matthew agreed. "Cratchit children, back on stage, please."

The rest of the rehearsal finished without incident, but keeping his gaze away from Holly Chamberlain nearly drove Grayson to distraction. Spending time with Priscilla Honeywell–pretty enough, mind you and a good actress to boot–just to get a new roof for St. Martin's seemed a bit much.

But the roof *was* in bad shape, with several leaks, the biggest one being right over the pulpit. If being a bit friendly—and only a very little bit, mind you—got St. Martin's a new roof, then Grayson would do his best.

He shoved his hands in his pockets and watched forlornly as Theo Barrett helped Holly into her coat, called his goodbyes to everyone, and started to lead her out of the parish hall. His hand curled around a scrap of cloth, his fingertips finding a bit of lace along the edge.

"Miss Chamberlain!" He found himself darting toward her, ignoring the frown that seemed to be a permanent feature of Theo Barrett's face.

But her eyes brightened as he stopped before them, and her smile was enough to tempt a man to do just about anything. "Yes, Mr. Clark?"

"You forgot this." He held out her handkerchief. "I mistakenly put it in my pocket."

"How very kind of you," she said, taking it from him. "Thank you."

"There you are, Mr. Clark." Priscilla Honeywell's voice behind Grayson interrupted any further conversation. "Grandpapa's carriage is here and he doesn't like the horses to get cold. Shall we go?"

"My friend needs another letter," Grayson said suddenly, looking at Holly. "Might I call on you Monday at three o'clock?" *Even if I get to see you at tomorrow's rehearsal, it's not the same as being alone with you. At least I'll get to kiss you again then.*

Her eyes widened. "Was the first one successful?"

"Immensely so," Grayson said, offering up a silent prayer for forgiveness. *It isn't really a lie, Lord, but a future truth. At least I hope it will be. Might I have a little help from You in this matter?*

"If you wish," she said, placing her gloved hand on Theo's arm. "Three o'clock Monday afternoon."

"Monday afternoon," Grayson repeated, watching the elegant pair depart the room. A gentle throat clearing reminded him of the young woman by his side, and holding back a sigh, Grayson turned to give his attention to Miss Priscilla Honeywell.

Chapter Four

"'As countless are the stars in the heavens, none have the brilliance of your eyes. Neither does the brightest of diamonds match it. One look from you and I am stunned into silence, tongue-tied, unable to force even the smallest of words from my lips. But know this, dearest of ladies, one word from you, and I am yours forever.'"

Grayson looked up from the page lying on Miss Chamberlain's desk. To hold it would give away the trembling of his hands. "What do you think?"

Those brilliant eyes sparkled back at him. "Your friend is obviously a student of Shakespeare," she commented.

"Why do you say that?"

"'Brevity is the soul of wit,'" she quoted. "Or to paraphrase, in declaring one's love. And in this case, saying just enough and not going on and on and on is far more effective in getting the point across than pages and pages of praise."

"I shall tell him you think so," Grayson promised, silently congratulating himself for running out of words. "May I read the next one?"

"Yes, indeed." Miss Chamberlain put aside the filled page and reached for a blank sheet of paper from the stack. "You may begin, Mr. Clark."

Grayson cleared his throat. "Ah, there is one other thing, Miss Chamberlain."

"Yes?"

Dear Lord, if this isn't a good idea, please shut me up now. "Since we are spending so much time together in rehearsals, would you think it too forward of me to ask you to call me by my Christian name?"

Color flooded her face, and Grayson's heart sank. "Oh, dear," he said. "I've offended you. I do beg your pardon."

Her sudden soft laugh erased his fears. "Not at all," she said. "I was hoping you would ask me that very thing. After all, we are friends, after a fashion, are we not? Friends call each other by their given names. I will call you Grayson if you promise to call me Holly."

"I would be honored to name you as my friend," Grayson said. "If you don't think your father will mind."

She wrinkled her nose. "Papa is far too forward thinking to mind such a thing."

"Good," Grayson declared, with an inward sigh of relief. "Good."

"And now for your friend's third letter?"

Nodding, Grayson took out another sheet of paper from his folder and squinted at it. "I really must say something to my friend about his handwriting."

"You must be a friend indeed if you can make out his squiggles," she said playfully.

"One can only hope," Grayson said. "Let me see. 'Your smile's warmth is more than a thousand suns, and yet I am not burned. To stand in its glow is all one could hope for, for it brings me into your radiance, and being so close, brings me joy, fairest and most beloved of ladies.'"

He read very slowly, pausing to give her time to write down his words. The only other sound than the scratching of pen against paper came from the tall clock in the corner, the silent chirp of the second hand whispering away the seconds. Holly's fingers curled around the pen and she had to swallow hard before saying, "I do believe that it is quite the loveliest thing I've ever heard."

"He means it most sincerely."

Holly lifted her gaze from the paper before her to find Grayson's amber eyes staring intently at her. "I hope his lady responds in kind," she said at last. "You are sure he is a man of good character?"

"He tries to be." A husky note had entered Grayson's voice. "A man can only do his best. Holly, I— that is to say—"

The door banged opened without so much as a knock, and Theo Barrett strode inside. Flakes of snow rested on the shoulders of his black overcoat and he dusted them off with a leather gloved hand.

"Sorry to interrupt, Grayson," he said casually, pulling up a chair to Holly's desk. "But I've news for Holly that won't wait."

"Well then, tell us!" Holly sent what she hoped was a sympathetic glance in Grayson's direction.

The barrister's chest seemed to swell by at least six inches. "I've been made a partner in the firm of Hinkle, Tyler and Ellis," he boasted. "Youngest man ever to do so!"

"Theo, that's wonderful!" Holly did not have to pretend to sound proud of him. He *was* a nice man, even if he was a bit stuffy and opinionated. He was a barrister after all, and a very nice-looking one too. But somehow Holly could not see him acting as a messenger for a lovelorn friend.

"And so I've come to take you to the Palm Court for high tea to celebrate," Theo continued. "You'll understand, won't you Grayson, if I steal her away from you?"

"Perfectly." Grayson rose and bowed to Holly. "I thank you again for assisting my friend, Miss Chamberlain. Congratulations, Theo. I'm sure you'll do well. Good afternoon to you both."

Oh dear. He didn't call me Holly. Perhaps he'd rather Theo find out we're calling each other by our names at the next rehearsal.

"Thank you, Mr. Clark," she called after his departing figure. "I'll see you tomorrow night at the rehearsal."

He pivoted, and the expression in his eyes showed he shared her thoughts about Theo. Theo was a dear, but would stand on ceremony.

"Yes, we will," Mr. Clark affirmed with a nod. "And as Christmas is next week, my friend may need another letter or two. That is, if you have the time."

"I'll make the time," Holly assured him. "How could I say no to one who writes such endearing statements to his lady?"

"I'll tell him you said so." The clergyman gave the briefest of bows, and left them alone.

"He's an odd duck, don't you think? Theo asked. "Never knew anyone like him."

"He's a modern man, Theo, even if he is a clergyman," Holly scolded gently. "Not all pompous and full of himself like Obadiah Slope in Mr. Thackery's novel."

"Who?"

Holly held back her sigh. "Never mind." She looked down at her desk, and gasped, "Oh my goodness. He left his friend's letters!"

She grabbed the sheets, tucked them inside the folder, and raced from the room and into the foyer. There was no sign of him. Grabbing her coat from the rack in the corner, she darted outside, scanning the neighborhood. She spotted him walking slowly down the sidewalk towards the corner, head down, his hands in his coat pockets. "Grayson, " she called.

He spun about, and upon seeing her, his face lit up. He matched her speed in returning to meet her in the middle of the sidewalk.

"You forgot this." Holly held out the folder.

"How silly of me," he said, taking it from her. "I suppose I thought Theo wanted me gone as quickly as possible."

"You mustn't disappoint your friend," Holly teased.

"Not for the world," he agreed.

They laughed together, and Holly thought frantically of something to say, to keep them together even for a moment. "Look," she said, choosing the safest of topics. "It's snowing. Do you like snow, Grayson?"

"Yes. When I was growing up in the Kent countryside, my brother and sisters and I lived near a large hill, and we had great fun sledding down it. We built snow forts too, and would stay inside them for hours at a time."

"I've always lived in the city," Holly admitted. "Sledding down a hill sounds like great fun."

"It was." Grayson's gaze on her face was sending the most delicious warmth coursing through her. He really did have the most amazing eyes, amber-colored and full of light, and she shivered at the memory of him kissing her at rehearsals.

But then he said, "I mustn't keep you and I do need to get these letters to my friend. I'll see you at the next rehearsal, Holly."

He held out his gloved hand, and she accepted it, feeling a surprising strength in his palm and fingers, and the earlier warmth became a flow of heat, surging through her. Standing with him beneath the swirling snow, Holly would not have moved for the world.

But then he broke the spell by releasing her hand, raising two fingers to the brim of his hat in salute, and departed, leaving Holly to stare after his tall figure. She wasn't sure if the sudden tears pricking her eyes were from the snow or the certain knowledge that the letters would soon be delivered to Priscilla Honeywell. In spite of all Holly's advantages, her father was after all "in trade," and men, as everyone knew, always wanted to "marry up." How could she compete with a baronet's beautiful granddaughter? She should be grateful for Theo's attentions. Marrying Holly was certainly to *his* advantage as his father was only a solicitor in a small firm.

"Blast, she muttered as she began her return to the waiting Theo. "Why must love be so complicated?"

Chapter Five-🍂

"Places!" Matthew shouted. Everyone on stage for the Cratchit family's scene!"

It was two days before Christmas Eve, and Grayson's duties at work had kept him at St. Martin's. So much so there had been no time to think of composing the last two letters to Holly, much less return to her office and have her write them out.

And of course, he was trying his very best to respond to Priscilla Honeywell's gentle flirtation. It must be working, for he had dined no less than four times with her parents in the last six days. He had increased his daily walk by two miles just to work off the richness of the Honeywell table.

But recalling Tobais Small's visit to the rectory last evening, Grayson suppressed a shudder. Small's gleeful attitude suggested a check for St. Martin's new roof was about to be deposited in the bank.

"Good work, my boy!" he had praised. "I know of course you can't do much until Advent is over as far as proposing to her. But Honeywell tells me his granddaughter has always wanted a Valentine's Day wedding, so you have plenty of time to take care of things."

Marry Priscilla Honeywell? That had certainly not been part of the bargain.

"All right, Cratchits! I've a new twist to add to your scene." Matthew stood in front of the stage, arms akimbo. He waited patiently as the various Cratchit children took their places."I've just learned that our Freddie–or should I say our Peter Cratchit–plays the squeezebox. So in the family scene, we're going to add a little dancing to the convivial atmosphere. Holly, Grayson, you know how to dance, don't you?"

"You want us to dance together?" Holly gasped.

"I say, is that really necessary?" Theo protested.

"I want people to see the love the Cratchits have for each other," Matthew growled. "Who's directing this play, I ask?"

"I know how to dance," Grayson affirmed. "Is it to be a waltz, Freddie? Or a jig?"

"I can do both," Freddie said proudly, holding up the squeezebox. "What do you want me to play, Mr. Timmons?"

"Let's start with a jig," Matthew said. "Holly and Grayson will start by dancing with the other children, then segue into a waltz. Let's get started. I'll cue you, Freddie."

Never in Grayson's wildest imaginings had he dreamed of dancing with Holly Chamberlain, much less holding her in his arms. But when the time came, Freddie changed the lively jigs and reels into a slow, stately waltz. The children dropped back, and Grayson bowed to his partner. "Mrs. Cratchit," he intoned loudly, "might I have the honor of this dance?"

She caught his mood and made a deep curtsy. "You may indeed, Mr. Cratchit."

The children giggled as they came together and Grayson swept Holly in carefully controlled movements about the parish hall stage. Her long, slender fingers curled around his, and in her smile he found all he could want.

"You dance beautifully, Mrs. Cratchit," he praised, not knowing what else to say and not daring to say more, lest he give his heart away in front of everyone.

"As do you, my love," she answered, and the children laughed again.

"Look, Tim, Mama and Papa are dancing," Clara/Martha said.

"Hurrah!" Dick/Tim cried, beating the floor with his crutch.

The entire cast—except Theo—burst into laughter and applauded as the too brief waltz came to an end. Grayson gave a theatrical bow and kissed Holly's hand. "Well done, my dear!" he said.

"Oh, that's good, that's very good!" Matthew called. "Am I brilliant, or am I brilliant?"

"You're brilliant," the cast answered dutifully.

"Well then, let's go on," Matthew said, taking the pencil from behind his ear and making a note on the tattered script pages. "We start where Scrooge says. . ."

By evening's end and to everyone's relief, Matthew announced they needed only one more rehearsal, in full dress, to polish things up.

"You've all been splendid," he praised the cast. "And a special thanks to the children and their parents, for being such troopers. Don't forget, curtain goes up here on Christmas Eve at five o'clock, so everyone needs to be here by three. Now, Mrs. Allen, little Dick's mother, and Sir Cyrus our patron, have not only put up refreshments for us tonight, but will do so after the play to celebrate our production, and Miss Honeywell's approaching twenty-first birthday. So let's enjoy ourselves. I for one, need a cup of tea."

The assembly headed for the stairs in back of the stage, men to the left, ladies to the right. Grayson watched Holly depart with the other women, enjoying the sway of her old-fashioned skirt. With a sigh, he headed backstage to change clothing. At the bottom of the stairs, Grayson spotted Theo talking with Oliver Simpson who played Scrooge's nephew Fred, and he ducked behind a large stack of boards piled in the shadows.

"I'll pick up the ring on Christmas Eve, and propose to Holly on Christmas Day evening," Theo said. "Her father always has an open house then and I thought that would be the perfect time."

"Couldn't have chosen a better woman for a wife," Oliver said. "You're quite sure she'll say yes?"

"I wouldn't have bought the ring if I weren't, old man," Theo boasted.

Heart sinking, Grayson waited until they headed back into the Parish Hall. He had two days until Christmas Eve to come up with the right words for the last letters to Holly. But try as he might, no words were coming. Writing his Christmas Eve's sermon had been far easier than this. He would have to force his brain into action before Theo put the ring on Holly's finger.

He entered the Parish Hall and spied his beloved standing with Miss Honeywell and her grandfather. Sir Cyrus beamed and waved to Grayson to join them.

"Good work, Grayson," he boomed. "Splendid portrayal of Bob Cratchit."

"Thank you, Sir Cyrus," Grayson said, trying not to gulp as Miss Honeywell came to stand as close to him as manners would allow and not look improper. She batted her eyelashes at him with such rapidity, Grayson wasn't sure if she were trying to flirt, or if she had something in her eyes.

"I do believe that Grayson's portrayal is quite poignant," she cooed, actually laying her hand on his arm.

"Grandpapa, do say I might invite Grayson to share Christmas Day dinner with us."

"Anything you want, my dear," Sir Cyrus said, giving Grayson a wide smile.

Grayson's heart sank again. *Why do I have a feeling that its <u>my</u> goose that's about to be roasted and presented on the Honeywell table for Christmas dinner?*

Chapter Six-❧

"And God bless us, every one!" the cast shouted at the crowd packing St. Martin's parish hall to overflowing. Wild applause broke out as they came forward, holding hands to take their bows. The children earned their own huge round of cheers and whistles as did the rest of those filling the cast's minor roles.

When Holly and Grayson stepped to the edge of the stage, he took her hand and bowed to her. She followed with a curtsy and the applause grew in its strength.

They stepped back, and Theo Barrett stepped up to receive a thunderous ovation from the gathering. He nodded and smiled and motioned for Matthew to join them for still more applause. Then the curtain came down, and the cast scattered, eager to be with friends and family. Grayson looked for Holly, but she was gone. As she would be by this time tomorrow afternoon. Gone from him forever.

And he would be dining with Miss Honeywell and her grandfather.

At least he had come up with two short missives and made it to Holly's office for her to write them out late this morning. He sighed, thinking of his poor, short attempts at putting his heart on paper.

There is none like you, fairest of ladies. One moment, one hour by your side, hearing the sound of your beloved voice protects me and surrounds me with such riches, that I am in all amazement. You hold my heart in your hand, and there I would rest forever.

He dare not think of the last one. Cheeks burning, he left the empty stage. Behind the same boards where he had hidden himself to listen to Theo and Oliver, he heard a giggle and then a whisper and then—Merciful Heavens!

"Oh no," Priscilla Honeywell whispered, breaking her kiss with a wide-eyed, astonished Matthew Timmons.

"I say, Grayson, be a good fella and don't betray us," Matthew pleaded.

At first Grayson could only stare. "B-but Miss Honeywell. I thought that you—"

"I'm sorry to break your heart, Grayson, but I had to pretend I was in love with you until my birthday because Grandpapa would never have permitted me to marry Matthew." Priscilla's words came out in a rush. "But now that I'm twenty-one and have come into my own money and–"

His heart beating in wild exaltation, Grayson held up his hand to stop her. "You may marry and still inherit. I quite understand. You plan to elope? Right now?" The pair nodded and Grayson said, "What about your grandfather, Miss Honeywell?"

"He's singing solo at all the services at St. Alban's tonight," she said. "He'll be too busy to notice I'm not there until it's too late."

"Then go quickly, and may God bless you both," Grayson said in his best pulpit voice.

The couple hurried away, and hope returned to Grayson's heart. Returning to the parish hall, he scanned it for Holly, who was of course, standing with Theo. For a moment, the look she gave the barrister nearly changed Grayson's mind, but a man must do what he must. Spying Clara talking with Oliver, he hurried to join them and said, "A private word with you, Miss Clara?"

He tugged at her sleeve and pulled her into a corner before she could answer. Eyes wide, she said, "Whatever is the matter, Mr. Clark?"

"I need your help on a matter most urgent," he said. "What time does Miss Holly get up on Christmas Day?"

She wrinkled her nose at him. "Right around six to prepare her Papa's special breakfast. The bread has to soak in the milk and sugar mixture before we cook it. Why?"

"Because—" and Grayson leaned over to whisper in her ear.

Her eyes filled with tears. "Oh, sir," she whispered. "That's the most romantic—"

"Hush," he whispered back. "Do you understand what you need to do?"

She nodded and after making sure Holly's attention was on her coachman Harold–who had grown out old-fashioned mutton chop whiskers to play their Fizziwig–Grayson hurried backstage, found his coat and hat and left St. Martin's for Chestnut Street.

Chapter Seven-🍂

"Merry Christmas, Miss Holly," Clara greeted as Holly entered the kitchen.

"Merry Christmas, Clara," Holly echoed, taking the traditional cup of cocoa. She quickly drank it and asked, "Is the milk for the bread pudding good and cold?"

"Yes, Miss, but before we start, could you go and hang up the stockings on the mantle? Some have fallen down, and I can't find the hammer."

"It's on the mantle, but I'll go do it," Holly said, giving her the cup. She headed toward the parlor and from behind the slightly open door, saw the shimmer of firelight. She pushed back the door and gasped.

Two filled candelabras stood on either side of the mantle, from where five embroidered stockings hung, each bearing an initial of her name. She stumbled forward and saw each held a scroll of paper. Hands trembling, she took out and unrolled the paper from the H stocking. She gasped again as her own handwriting greeted her. *Since the moment of our first meeting…* but the signature was that of her beloved, Grayson Clark. From the O to the second L, all the stockings contained the letters she had written to his dictation, and all signed by him.

Tears running down her cheeks, she pulled out the remaining scroll, remembering their laughter at his 'friend's combining borrowed lines from Jane Austen's *Persuasion* and one of Shakespeare's sonnets. *Oh, how I faint, when I of you do write, for you pierce my soul. One glance from you and I am half hope, half despair. For I have loved and will always love none but you.*

Yours alone, Grayson Clark.

Grateful she always changed into her clothing before preparing Papa's Christmas breakfast, Holly dashed for the hall closet and her coat, and she was out the door, where miracle of miracles–for Christmas is after all, all about miracles–the family coach and driver waited. A smiling Harold helped her inside before climbing back on the box and setting the horses into motion.

And because it was a miracle, Holly didn't even have to tell him where to go.

The greenery hanging from the communion rail and pulpit scented the empty church. With a heavy heart, Grayson finished lighting the candles on the altar and returned to the sacristy. Christmas Day was here, and within minutes, the sexton would unlock the front door for the seven o'clock service. In the bell tower, the ringers had already gathered, waiting for the clock to strike the hour so they could set the bells into motion.

He'd always associated the scent of evergreen with hope, but it was foolish to hope that writing love letters to Holly Chamberlain would make a difference. By this afternoon, she would be engaged to Theo Barrett and that would be the end of it. After all, Grayson was only a clergyman and—

"Grayson." A beloved voice called from the doorway. Its owner hovered there, as if unsure if she should enter or flee. But the light in her eyes outshone the altar candles, and Grayson opened his arms to her. She ran to enfold herself against him and he buried his face in her glorious unbound hair.

"You found the stockings?" he asked.

"An Oxford scholar asks such a question?" she whispered. "You got Clara and Harold to help, didn't you?"

"Yes," he admitted sheepishly. "It was the only way. Dare I hope you're here—"

"Because I love you?" She lifted her head and in her eyes was the promise of love, tomorrows yet to come and all the happily-ever-afters one could dream of. "So much for you're being a scholar. Yes, silly man, because I love you. Only you."

"And here I was thinking you loved Theo," Grayson sighed in relief.

"And I thought you were in love with Priscilla," Holly said. "It nearly broke my heart thinking those letters were for her."

"Good thing they weren't, or Matthew would have killed me," and Grayson told her about the by now newlywed couple.

She laughed. "So there we were, writing and dreaming of the one we loved when they were just across the desk. A fine pair we made."

"A fine pair we'll make," Grayson corrected, kissing her forehead. "What about Theo?"

"He'll have to find someone else," Holly said. "Is it a sin to kiss in the sacristy?"

"I'll have to ask the bishop," Grayson said, pulling her closer. "But it's a good place for a proposal."

She pretended to pout. "But I was going to propose to you."

"Then let's ask each other together. On the count of three. One, two…"

"Marry me, Grayson?"

"Marry me, Holly?"

"Yes," they chorused and above them the bells began to peal out *Joy to the World*, spreading the news to all of London that Christmas Day was indeed finally here.

But wrapped in each others' arms, Grayson and Holly, were too busy enjoying the first of a lifetime of kisses to notice.

The Christmas Proposal

The Christmas Proposal

London December 1897

"You said no to a proposal from Viscount Ramsfield's son?" Great aunt Tilda Mason's shrieked words rivaled a banshee's cry. "Quick, Hildegarde. My smelling salts!"

From her place by the fire, Cassandra Barnwell watched the lady's maid rush forward, the ever-ready bottle of Crayfield's smelling salts in her hand. It was a great pity Cassandra had never invested in Crayfield's. With the number of times her great aunt called for them each day, Cassandra's fortune would be twice as large at it was.

Of course if Aunt Tilda would just loosen her stays and get more exercise, her old friend the vapors would probably leave on a permanent holiday.

"There, there, ma'am," Hildegarde soothed, waving the bottle below Aunt Tilda's nose. "You'll soon be as right as rain."

"I'll probably die from palpitations by tomorrow," Aunt Tilda wailed. "Tell me why, Cassandra. Why did you say no?"

Feeling like a Jane Austen heroine, Cassandra said, "Because in spite of being a Viscount's son, Edward Ramsfield has nothing else to recommend him. He is quite opposed to women winning the vote and said if suffragists had husbands and homes to attend to, they would give up the notion of voting. Ergo, my refusal."

"Mercy, you didn't try to speak Latin to him?" Aunt Tilda clutched at her lace-covered bosom.

"If I had, I doubt he'd have understood a word of it," Cassandra said matter-of-factly. "Edward Ramsfield may be a Viscount's son, but he's a perfect dunce, and that's being kind. I'm surprised he finished at Harrow, much less university."

"Cassandra!"

Holding back her sigh of impatience, Cassandra said, "Hildegarde, why don't you make Aunt Tilda a tisane or something that will calm her?"

"Yes, Miss Barnwell." The maid pocketed the bottle, gave a quick curtsey and left the room.

"I don't know what I'm going to do with you," Aunt Tilda fretted, sitting up on the enormous horsehair sofa. "Christmas is only weeks away and announcing your engagement then would be so romantic. I do my best to introduce you to eligible young men, and you always find something wrong with them."

That's because they're all fortune hunters, my dear Aunt, with no interest in me except the number of zeros in my dowry. "Uncle Bob says they're making bets at all the gentlemen's clubs on whether I'll ever accept a proposal. Of course, they're just wasting their money. I don't think I shall ever marry."

"Cassandra Yvonne Barnwell!" Her aunt's wail returned.

"Look, here's Hildegarde back again." Cassandra said with more cheerfulness than she felt.

The maid's speedy return with the tisane suggested it was already made with its usual dose of Lydia Pinkham's Cordial added to it, a remedy that always put Aunt Tilda to sleep.

And as usual, soon after drinking it, Aunt Tilda's head began to droop, and within minutes the snore she always denied was thundering through the room. Hildegarde pulled the blanket from the back of the sofa and draped it over the tiny form. She flashed her familiar grin at Cassandra and said, "I think she'll sleep at least until tea, Miss."

"You're an angel, Hildegarde," Cassandra praised. "If anyone calls, I'm going to see Aunt Laura."

"Another suffragists' meeting?" Hildegarde guessed.

"Not today. We're going to see a new exhibit at the British Museum. But we've already started to plan a large rally in Hyde Park for after the New Year."

Hildegarde's grin broadened. "Your Aunt Laura is a caution."

Cassandra smiled in return at the thought of Laura Barnwell, her beloved Uncle Bob's wife and president of the local chapter of Women United for Equality. "She is indeed. Aunt Laura says all women need to be involved in the suffrage movement. After all, the laws Parliament passes apply to us, so why shouldn't we have be able to vote for them?"

"Or against them," Hildegarde said earnestly.

"Or against them," Cassandra agreed. "If Aunt Tilda asks, I took a cab to Aunt Laura's instead of walking. She'll have another 'fit' and I think that was the last bottle of smelling salts in the house. But I'll be back by teatime."

Going to the door, she peeked into the foyer to be sure it was empty of any servant activity before fetching the coat and hat she kept in the front closet. Before putting them on, she stopped at the wall mirror long enough to be sure her barely controlled auburn hair had not escaped its pins and frown at her reflection. Despite a twice daily application of fading cream, the long detestable freckles still dotted her cheeks and bridged her nose. Not even buttermilk had done the trick.

"With a face and hair like that, of course my money is the only reason men want to court me," she told her reflection as she put on her hat. "Only a man in the most desperate of situations would even consider such a thing."

Shrugging into her coat, Cassandra opened the door and stepped outside the Grosvenor Square mansion. A light snow whispered around her, covering the ground with a fine, white powder. In the distance, a carillon chimed *I Heard the Bells on Christmas Day* and from near by wafted the scent of roasting chestnuts. All signs that Christmas was not far away.

"A Christmas wedding," she sighed again and a curious wistfulness settled around her heart. "Even if I've been very, *very* good, that's about as likely as a visit from Father Christmas."

Lengthening her stride, she headed for the corner.

***

"Ah, Brandon, here you are at last." The bearded man behind the desk clambered to his feet. "Welcome home from Egypt, my lord. When did you return?"

Lord Brandon Russell crossed the artifact-cluttered room in the British Museum to shake his university friend's outstretched hand. "You can save the 'my lord' for my brother, Albert. I got off the boat from Fort Said an hour ago."

Albert Graham, the Museum's curator of Asian antiquities waved Brandon into a chair. "Home for Christmas, are you?"

Brandon sank gratefully into the chair's upholstered depths and crossed his legs. "That and my younger sister Gwendolyn's wedding on New Year's Day."

"I remember seeing the announcement in the London *Times*," Albert said, "The sister of a duke marrying another duke's heir. I'm sure His Grace is pleased."

"That alone would have made the *Times*," Brandon said dryly. "Considering how seldom Trevor is pleased by anything."

Albert's eyebrows rose. "Is the Duke of Halstead still annoyed at you for—how did he put it—'digging up crockery in the desert' instead of taking your rightful place in Society?"

"Something like that," Brandon admitted. "Communication between us is sparse at best. Gwendolyn keeps me informed of family matters."

"His Grace has very particular ideas about your family, doesn't he?"

"Yes." Brandon said wearily. "And they don't include me living in the Egyptian desert nine months out of the year or funding my expeditions. Thanks to my father's will, the bulk of my inheritance is tied up until I turn thirty-two or marry. I have no intention of the latter, which is why I must rely on funding from the British Museum. What contributions Trevor occassaionly makes hardly get me to Gibraltar, let alone Egypt. As he so frequently reminds me, until Mother Nature takes a hand, and gifts him with a son, *I* am his heir and should act accordingly. Which includes getting married."

Albert shot him a wicked grin. "The younger brother of a duke-particularly one who only has daughters-*would* be considered quite a catch for many a wealthy young woman."

"How many young women do you know who would willingly live in a canvas tent with sand and camels for companions?" Brandon made no attempt to hide his sarcasm. "Let's not even talk about the windstorms or the snakes."

"There's something to be said for bachelorhood," Albert agreed. "No one to tell you what to do, how to do it, and when to come home."

"My point exactly," Brandon said. "Speaking of Gibraltar, did you get the telegram I sent from there? The one about next year's funding?"

"Ah, well- Yes. Yes I did."

Albert's expression switched from one of pleasant bonhomie to that of a man just force-fed a lemon. Brandon leaned forward. "What is it?"

"All this talk about weddings," Albert hedged. "Who'd have thought . . ."

Suspicion coiled Brandon's stomach and he leaned forward. "What do weddings have to do with next year's funding?"

"I suppose you'll hear about it at one of your clubs," Albert sighed. "Old Reggie Cheswick got himself married to a chorus girl last week. And she has made it quite clear that any extra monies he has to spend are to be spent on *her*, not some expedition half way across the globe."

Brandon swore in three archaic languages before asking, "Then where am I going to get funds? Cheswick has been underwriting the dig for the past six years!"

Albert spread his hands in a gesture of apology. "I haven't a clue. Are you sure your brother won't help you?"

"Quite." Brandon bit off the word. "And I'm close, Albert. So close to a major discovery."

"I'm sorry," Albert said. "But don't despair yet. It's almost Christmas. What do you say I invite some of the Museum's contributors to a little dinner and see if we can shake some funds loose?"

"Whatever works." Brandon sat back again. "I'm obliged to you."

"Not at all." Albert declared. "Now, before you go, let me show you the new Egyptian history exhibit. We've used some of the artifacts you discovered along with the loaned ones you sent from the Cairo museum."

He stood and Brandon followed him into the hall and the vast gallery that housed the Museum's Egyptian

Antiquities collection. Well-dressed people filled the area, stopping to talk with friends or gaze at the artifacts of Egyptian daily life. Brandon recognized the very large mummy case of a merchant he had personally found. "Everything looks splendid." he said.

"Thanks to you," Albert replied. "Well, bless my soul. There's a piece of good luck."

"What?"

Albert gestured at two women who stood looking at series of photographs of the Sphinx. "If you want a new funding source, you should try them."

Brandon stared at the subjects of their discussion. The taller woman had glossy black hair and a serene expression. Her companion was younger and even from across the room Brandon could not miss the twin copper curls framing her face. Her dress's simple elegance was all the proof he needed of her wealth.

As if she had read his mind, she turned and looked in his direction. Their gazes met and color brightened her face. Then she smiled, and its warmth hit Brandon with the force of a blow. "Who are they?" he asked.

"Mrs. Robert Barnwell and her niece Cassandra Barnwell.."

"Barnwell?" A sweet taste flooded Brandon's mouth. "Of Barnwell's Chocolates and Confections?"

"The very ones," Albert said. "They are often of a philanthropic nature. Mr. Barnwell fancies Greek artifacts more than Egyptian ones, but perhaps we could convince them otherwise. Shall I invite them to the dinner?"

And before Brandon could fashion a reply, Albert beckoned the women to join them. The older one nodded and they moved through the crowd with an eye-pleasing grace. They stopped and Mrs. Barnwell said, "Mr. Graham, how very nice to see you again. You remember my niece, Miss Cassandra Barnwell, of course?"

Albert smiled and said, "Of course. A pleasure to see you again, Miss Barnwell. Allow me to introduce my friend and colleague, Brandon Russell, fresh off the boat from Egypt. He found many of the objects you see around you. Brandon, this is Mrs. Robert Barnwell and her niece Miss Cassandra Barnwell."

"Welcome home, Mr. Russell." Miss Barnwell held out her gloved hand and he took it. Her soft husky voice sent a ripple of pleasure over Brandon's skin. So did her touch.

Grateful that Albert had not included his title in his introduction, Brandon bowed to them. "Ladies, I'm delighted. I'm sorry to say that Barnwell's Chocolates and Confections are not easily found in Egypt and I have sorely missed them."

Mrs. Barnwell favored him with a smile. "Aren't they? Perhaps we should make you our Egyptian agent. Then we could keep you well supplied."

"We should open a factory there, Aunt Laura," Miss Barnwell suggested. "Otherwise the chocolates would melt on the way."

The men laughed. "An excellent point, Miss Barnwell." Albert conceded.

"I'm a peppermint man, myself," Brandon added. "Less danger of melting, don't you think?"

"Ah, then you must try our chocolate covered peppermints," Miss Barnwell countered. Her eyes, dark as the chocolates she boasted of, twinkled as she added, "They are not to be missed. We can have a box sent to you as a welcome home present if you like."

"I should like that," Brandon said and her smile warmed his skin again. She wasn't exactly a beauty but she had a certain appealing presence. And who had told her to cover up those freckles with face powder?

"Lord Brandon! Lord Brandon!" A strident feminine voice broke into their conversation and its owner, purple plumes waving from her oversized hat sailed forward. Miss Barnwell's eyes widened, and she stepped back before being mowed over by the very large woman in an equally purple dress.

"Lady Stanhope." Brandon forced a smile. Of all the people to see his first hour home in London why must it be Lucille Stanhope? Her daughter Millicent had not so subtly pursued him the last time he was home. Judging from Lady Stanhope's enthusiasm, Millicent must still be in the market for a husband.

"Welcome home, my lord," Lady Stanhope gushed. "How does your brother? I hope His Grace and his Duchess are well?"

"I've only just arrived home," Brandon reluctantly admitted. He could lie and say he'd been home a week, but sooner or later she'd learn he was being less than truthful. Her ability to ferret things out made Sherlock Holmes look like a rank amateur. "I hope to find my brother and his family in good health."

The woman's pebble gray eyes glittered in speculation. "You have no doubt returned for your sister's wedding?"

"No doubt," Brandon agreed. "Lady Lucille Stanhope, allow me to introduce Mrs.–"

"Do say you'll come to dinner while you're in town, Lord Brandon," Lady Stanhope cut him off without so much as a glance at the other women. Plucking a card from her handbag, she said. "I receive every afternoon between two and four. Millicent will be delighted to see you again. She's become quite the Egyptian scholar. I'll expect to hear from you."

With a deep curtsy, she turned and swept from the gallery like a man o' war, plumes still waving. After a moment's silence, Mrs. Barnwell asked, "Where would you like us to send the peppermints, Lord Brandon?"

Brandon shoved the card into a trouser pocket. "The Albany."

"The Albany it is, then. Come, Cassandra."

"A pleasure to have met you, Lord Brandon," Miss Barnwell said. The twinkle in her eyes sparkled back at him, while the smile hovering about the corners of her primly held mouth, suggested she was on the edge of bursting into laughter.

"The pleasure was all mine, Miss Barnwell." Brandon bowed again.

"Come Cassandra," Mrs. Barnwell said. "If I don't have you back in time for tea, your Great Aunt Tilda will make both our lives miserable. Especially since she's invited Lady DeMerle and her son."

Sighing, Miss Barnwell bowed her head as if waiting the deathblow. "You aren't going to leave me alone with them, are you, Aunt Laura?"

"Of course not, my dear. You won't have to face the matrimonial wolves alone. Good afternoon, gentlemen."

Linking her arm with her niece, Mrs. Barnwell led them away, vanishing into the increasing crowd.

"Well, there's the answer to your problems, Brandon," Albert said with a laugh once the women were out of earshot. "You can marry Lady Millicent Stanhope. As an earl's son-in-law, you'd have more than enough money to bankroll your expeditions for years."

"I'd rather sleep with a pit viper," Brandon growled.

"Then perhaps you could marry Miss Barnwell," Albert suggested, still grinning. "No title, but lots and lots of money. Of course, you'll have lots of competition. Her fortune's said to run to six figures and Christmas weddings are currently all the rage."

"Since when did you start playing matchmaker?" Brandon asked. "Now, you'll excuse me. If I don't put in an appearance at Halstead House, the duke will have my head displayed from the Tower by morning. Good to see you again, Albert. Let me know about the dinner."

And sighing inwardly, Brandon headed for the door.

***

"Poor Lord Brandon," Aunt Laura said as they traveled back to Grosvenor Square. "He'll have no rest if Lucille Stanhope has designs on him for her Millicent. That should please his brother, the Duke of Halstead. I should have remembered they are half-brothers."

Cassandra peered at her from the other seat. "What are you talking about, Aunt Laura?"

"You should pay more attention to Society gossip my dear, especially since so many of them patronize our stores," Aunt Laura teased. "It's a known fact the Duke of Halstead would prefer his half-brother and heir to stay in London instead of running around the globe and putting himself and the Halstead line in danger of dying out. Because of that, he refuses to finance Lord Brandon's work."

The image of the tall archeologist flooded Cassandra's memory and for some strange reason, her cheeks heated. His blond, collar-touching hair proved a barber was not available on his journey home, but his neatly pressed suit–from his shoulder hugging jacket and well fitting trousers falling from a slim waist down very long legs–suggested a valet's presence aboard ship. She cleared her throat and asked, "Really? Who does finance his work?"

"Until last week, it was Reginald Cheswick. Remember we've had a standing order for five pounds of chocolates a month from him for the past year. Last week Mr. Cheswick married the recipient of those chocolates, and now the former Miss Ruthie Mays, one of the Variety Theater's Razzle-Dazzle Girls, has convinced him to stop wasting his money on a man who spends his life–"Aunt Laura's alto voice rose to a falsetto–"'playing in the world's biggest sandbox'. But the order for the chocolates still stands."

"I'm surprised a Razzle-Dazzle Girl has the wit to call the Egyptian desert a sandbox," Cassandra said as the carriage turned down their street. "Poor Lord Brandon! Who will pay for his work now?"

Aunt Laura shook her head. "I've no idea. But the Duchess is advancing in her latest pregnancy. The clubs are betting she's carrying twins. Perhaps this time there will be an heir and a spare, and the Duke so overcome with happiness, he'll help Lord Brandon."

A giggle crossed Cassandra's lips. "Or Lord Brandon could marry Millicent Stanhope."

"He could," Aunt Laura laughed. "Oh goodness. Look." She pointed at the window as the carriage rolled to a stop.

Cassandra's heart sank. Aunt Tilda must have discovered her tisane was drugged, because her revenge was apparent in the not one, not two, but three carriages, doors emblazoned with family crests, standing before the house. Bachelors. Fortune hunting bachelors.

"Oh, Aunt Tilda," Cassandra moaned. "What have you done ?"

***

"If perhaps you'd discovered something *monumental,* I might consider endowing you," Trevor Russell, Duke of Halstead said dryly. "But your disregard for your own safety and the possible ending of the Halstead line only doubles the reason I cannot endow you."

You make me sound like I'm nothing more than a breeding stallion. It's a damn shame medical science isn't advanced enough to determine the gender of a child before he or she is born, then you'd know if your next one will be the heir you desire so much. Brandon pushed aside the glass of port on the table. "The archeological community has no doubts as to my discoveries' worth."

Trevor shrugged. "If you say so. I've never understood your passion for science, Brandon. Don't you care about your family history and reputation?"

Fighting the urge to roll his eyes–a gesture he knew Trevor despised–Brandon said, "Of course I do. Father certainly imbued us both with it. But a man has to have something to occupy his time. I had no desire for the army or the church, so why not science?"

"There are more gentlemanly pursuits than living out of a suitcase. Can't one of your friends find you an advisory position at a museum?"

"You just can't countenance the idea of me *working* for my living," Brandon pointed out. "Why shouldn't I be paid for it?"

"A duke's heir doesn't–."

"Yes, I know." Brandon sighed. "A duke's heir doesn't work for a living. This is an old argument, Trevor, and neither of us are likely to change our minds."

"Well, then." Trevor flicked a microscopic piece of dust from his dinner jacket. "As long as you make yourself available for Gwendolyn's engagement celebrations. Don't let me keep you from your evening, Brandon."

Glad for the dismissal, Brandon rose and left the library. Outside Halstead House, he walked the short distance to the corner and a cabstand. A blanketing fog shrouded the streetlights and he shivered. Even after years of nights in the desert, he always forgot how very bone chilling the November evenings in London could be.

He gave the driver the address for the Four-in-Hand Club and climbed inside the cab. Brandon didn't race, but the Russells had been among the club's founding members during the early days of the Regency, and it was a sure place to hear useful information. Information his late mother would have laughingly called gossip.

As to be expected during the approaching holiday season, the club was full of gentlemen who had stopped by before going to other engagements. His appearance brought a burst of applause from the assembly in the Blue Room. The number of bottles on the tables showed they were already deep in their cups.

"Speak of the Devil and there he is!" shouted one above the din of voices.

"I'll put in ten more quid if *he* can pull it off," another called. "London's most eligible bachelor and most unlikely to marry, will wed by New Year's."

"He'll have to marry after his sister's wedding, Freddie," corrected the first one. "But I'll gladly take your money, for there will be ice-skating in hell before you'll see Lord Brandon Russell at the altar."

Brandon scowled at the pair. He remembered both Freddie Vandergild and Bertie St. John from university, and the following years had not endowed them with any greater wisdom. Not that they had any to start. "Since when are my matrimonial prospects of such interest?"

"Oh, we're just making bets with the most impossible odds we can think of." Bertie held up a brandy filled snifter. "I've found a new pair of trotters and the old man won't free up my next six month's allowance. Said after my recent bad luck at the tables, I don't deserve it. Your getting engaged is the most outlandish thing we could think of. I just need to find someone to bet against me, for it would be a sure victory for me. "

"Oh I say, and I know just the candidate for him." Freddie gave Brandon a glassy-eyed grin. "Who's that little freckle-faced thing who's rolling in money and just said 'no' to Edward Ramsfield?"

"Cassandra Barnwell!" shouted Bertie. "By Jove, that's the ticket. Ramsfield must be desperate if he'd offer for her. Who'll bet against me? Twenty pounds says that no matter how she tries, Cassandra Barnwell's money won't snare Brandon Russell!"

"It's a good thing she's got money, because that's all she has to offer," a third man said morosely. "Tried for her meself and she turned me down flat."

"You're father's only a baronet, Roger," Bertie called. "Got to be a little higher in the instep for the Barnwell girl. Who's in?"

A general chorus of betting broke out and Freddie plucked a pencil and paper from his pocket. "Place your bets, gents. One at a time, no reason to rush."

Brandon elbowed his way through the group, took the pencil from Freddie and broke it. "No one bets on the Russells," he said. "Not unless you want the dinner invitations from my brother to your family to stop."

"Oh, be a sport, Russell," Bertie sneered. "No reason to act like your brother. I'll tell you what. Winner divides the spoils with you. After all, the Duke isn't about to free up any of his own coin to help you out, is he? Consider it a Christmas present from your old friends. Not unless you surprise us all and *do* marry. Then we get to keep it. What do you say? Place your bets, gentlemen, place your bets. The night is hurrying on."

Any attempt to answer was drowned by the men's shouts and thoroughly weary, Brandon left for the Albany. This was turning out to be a hell of a Christmas Season.

***

You've lost your mind, girl. He'll be calling the authorities to drag you off to Bedlam where they'll lock you up and throw away the key. Cassandra stopped at the top of the Museum stairs and stared down the long corridor leading to the Egyptian exhibit. Why on earth did she think Lord Brandon would even be here? If he only arrived home yesterday, he was surely visiting family or friends.

But she had to speak to him. After Aunt Tilda's coup yesterday, desperate action was called for, and she had lain awake half the night, thinking over her plan. She only prayed Lord Brandon would see the logic of it, the benefit of it. It would quite simply, save them both. How could he possibly refuse such an offer?

Cassandra continued her progress through the again crowded gallery. Egypt was wildly popular just now. She personally found the pantheon of Egyptian gods and goddesses far more interesting than the Greeks or Romans. Their sinister nature appealed to her in a strange way. A quick glance showed a hallway off the main hall and gathering her courage, Cassandra slowly walked its length to stop before an open door with the word 'workroom' printed on it. She peeked inside and an inaudible sigh of appreciation escaped her.

Lord Brandon stood behind a large wooden table, his shirtsleeves rolled up and well past his elbows displaying a pair of tightly muscled forearms. A thoughtful expression covered his handsome features as he reached into a large box and pulled out a wrapped object. After carefully removing the paper, he held it up, and after a moment's scrutiny, put it aside and made note on a pad of paper. No wonder Lady Stanhope was eager to snare him for her daughter. He was quite simply, breathtaking. She sighed again.

He looked up and his eyes widened. "Miss Barnwell?"

"Good afternoon, Lord Brandon," Cassandra said, still hesitating in the doorway. "I hope I'm not disturbing your work?"

"Not at all. Please come in."

She stepped inside as he quickly rolled down his sleeves, buttoned the cuffs and pulled on a jacket from the back of a nearby chair. Coming from behind the table, he met her halfway and held out his hand. "I'm delighted to see you again, Miss Barnwell. Is Mrs. Barnwell with you?"

"No, I'm here by myself."

This time it was his eyebrows that rose in question over startlingly green eyes. "Is that wise Miss Barnwell? You being here without a chaperone?"

She smiled. "Aunt Laura won't mind. And my great Aunt Tilda spends her Wednesday afternoons doing charity work. I'll be home long before she is. I should like to speak with you about a private matter, if you don't mind."

"A private matter?" Brandon repeated and apprehension twisted his stomach. Young ladies did not usually call on gentlemen of a day's acquaintance without a chaperone to speak about "private matters." They did not even do so after six month's acquaintance. But somehow he suspected Cassandra Barnwell was not the usual young lady, and accustomed to getting what she wanted.

She looked quite striking today in her moss green coat and matching hat. The cold day had brightened her cheeks and intelligence shone in her dark, friendly eyes. No, Miss Cassandra Barnwell was not the typical young lady.

What could she possibly want from him?

"Perhaps we could go somewhere for tea?" she asked. "There's a shop around the corner.

"Very well. Just let me lock up."

A few minutes later found them seated at a table at Ivy's Tea Shop. After a smiling waitress took their order, Brandon looked at his companion and said, "So, Miss Barnwell. What is this private matter?"

"I'd like to hire you to court me."

Brandon coughed violently, grateful he didn't have a mouthful of tea. "You want to do what?" he gasped.

"Just that. I'd like to hire you to court me. You need the money, don't you?"

"Miss Barnwell, what the devil are you saying?" Good manners could go hang.

She sighed as if annoyed by his seeming incomprehension. "It's like this. My Great Aunt Tilda who means well, is the world's biggest matchmaker. She is obsessed with finding a husband for me and the specimens—"

"*Specimens?*"

Miss Barnwell frowned. "Oh, very well. I mean the *gentlemen*—and I hesitate to call them that—she brings forward as possible suitors are deplorable. She doesn't even ask me if I want to meet them. She springs them on me and I'm forced to have tea with them. Yesterday she surprised me with three. All were dreary, vapid and stupid. You, on my first observation, are none of those things."

"Thank you," Brandon said cautiously. "I think."

"You're welcome. Here is my plan. I know funding for your next venture has been cancelled. I know your brother the Duke of Halstead disapproves of your work and also refuses to invest in it. I'm prepared to invest in your next venture provided you court me seriously enough to convince Society of your sincere intent. I have access to my money, you see. Later on, I'll do something outrageous and you'll have to break off the courtship to spare your family's honor. You'll have your money and I'll be left alone, for no one would want to marry a woman whose behavior cost her a possible marriage to a duke's brother and heir."

She paused as the waitress brought their order, filled their cups and left. After drinking the entire contents of her cup, Miss Barnwell set it down and asked, "So what do you think?"

"I think you're mad." Brandon expelled a breath before taking a grateful sip of Earl Gray.

"I was afraid you'd say that." Miss Barnwell propped her elbows on the table and put her chin in her hands. "What's wrong with my idea?"

"Do you realize what you're asking? "

"Certainly," she affirmed with a quick nod. "You need a backer and I'm prepared to supply you with the funds you need. All you have to do is pretend to court me until–oh, say after Christmas when I'll do something outrageous and you'll break off the relationship. I'll pay you in advance of course."

Her matter of fact tone chilled Brandon. "Do you realize what you're asking?" he repeated. "You'd be ruined socially if *I* ended this so called courtship. A gentleman would never do that to a lady."

"He would if she did something like get arrested."

"Arrested?" Brandon quickly put down his cup before it tumbled from his hand.

"Oh, not for anything violent," she amended. "I was thinking more of disturbing the peace at next year's suffrage rally in Hyde Park. Your family would certainly disapprove of your courting a woman who did something like that."

"Is it your intent, then, never to marry?"

To his surprise, color flooded her face and she lowered her gaze. She fiddled with her spoon for a moment before saying, "I would if I thought a man wanted me for me and not just for my money. My parents married for love. So did my Uncle Bob and Aunt Laura. I refuse to marry for anything less than love." The tremble in her voice only added to his confusion.

"Miss Barnwell, I don't understand. Why shouldn't you be able to marry for love?"

She lifted her gaze from the tablecloth and he saw her eyes sparkling with unshed tears. "Lord Brandon–"

"Brandon," he corrected gently. "My friends call me Brandon."

Her color deepened to a rosy hue, but she smiled at him. "Brandon, then. Look at me. I have wildly red hair, a face full of freckles, am outspoken to the last degree, and I'm plump. I am hardly the kind of woman to inspire love or passion in a man. At least–" her voice trembled again, "–that's what I've overheard on more than one occasion. They call me *Freckles.*"

Plump? Trying not to stare, Brandon let his gaze travel over her. Miss Barnwell's figure was luscious. She held curves in all the places a woman should have them. True, she did not resemble the dainty, porcelain girls filling London ballrooms each Season, but Brandon had never wanted to hold porcelain in his arms. Too cold for one thing. And he had a particular fondness for freckles.

"So you see, it's the size of my dowry that attracts the suitors," she said with an air of finality. "Lots of zeros can inspire mock passion in a man. I know, for I've met a great many of them. But if scandal forces me off the marriage market, then the next time a man wants to court me, I will know it will be because he truly cares for *me.*"

Still amazed by her suggestion, Brandon asked, "And you would really do this? To insure a man's honest intent to court you?"

"I've no other way. Will you help me? Please?"

Brandon picked up his cup again, stalling for time. Her suggestion was wildly unorthodox and bordering on insanity.

And it just might work.

She would get the freedom to discern a man's honest courtship, and he would have a financial backer. All for just spending time with her and pretending to court her.

But what would happen after he was gone? Would she really be able to endure the censure that would follow her suggested plan for scandal? Only a rank coward would abandon her to such a fate, and Brandon was not a coward.

But still, to have his work endowed. "What did you have in mind, Miss Barnwell?"

Her expression brightened. "Why don't we start by you joining us at the opera tonight? Uncle Bob and Aunt Laura and I are going to see a special English production of *The Magic Flute* at the Lyceum with some friends. We're having a late supper at home afterwards and we have an extra ticket. That is, if you like opera."

"As a matter of fact, I do," Brandon said. "Very well. Are you sure your aunt and uncle won't mind?"

"Not at all. They trust me, you see."

"What about your matchmaking Great Aunt Tilda?"

Her laugh sent a wave of pleasure spiraling down his spine. "She will be so delighted that a duke's brother is courting me, she will send away all other callers," she said. "For that alone, I owe you thanks."

"Very well,'" he repeated. "What time shall I meet you at the Lyceum?"

"Seven-thirty," she said. "Thank you, Brandon. Oh, thank you."

She placed her gloved hand on his and warmth sparked through the silk and straight up his arm. The men of London must be suffering from collective stupidity not to see the charm in Miss Cassandra Barnwell. A faint warning bell rang in Brandon's head, but he only said, "I need to be getting back to work. Allow me to call you a cab."

He paid their bill and walked her outside. His whistle produced a cab and after she gave the driver her address, he helped her inside. He shut the door, bowed and said, "Until this evening, Miss Barnwell."

She smiled, lifted her hand in a gesture of farewell and the cab rolled away.

***

If I thought you handsome in your shirtsleeves, it was nothing compared to now, Cassandra's brain frantically searched for the memory of how to breathe.

In immaculate black and white evening clothes that sculpted his broad shoulders, flat belly and long legs to perfection, Brandon Russell had quite literally stopped all conversation when he moved across the lobby of the Lyceum to greet her and her party. Aunt Laura greeted him with the warmth of two old friends meeting again, and Uncle Bob accepted him as easily as if he met an aristocrat every day.

In their box she sat beside him, trying to concentrate on the music and not the faint scent of musk emanating from him, or the warmth radiating off his body. He was almost sinfully handsome, and more than once he turned his gaze away from the action on the stage and onto her. Her midnight blue gown showed a generous slope of shoulder, and more than a suggestion of a well-rounded bosom. For once in her life, Cassandra permitted herself the fantasy a man found her attractive. The thought heated her skin, but she kept the fan in her lap closed.

Now, back at her family's home, the evening was coming to an end. The other couples departed, but Brandon—should she really be thinking of him like that so soon?—remained seated, one long leg crossed over the other, listening to Uncle Bob's story about opening their seventh factory, this one in Dundee. His eyes flickered over to her, and a smile hovered around the corners of his mouth. A single bead of perspiration escaped from under her hair to trickle slowly down her neck

When Uncle Bob finished his story, their guest said, "I think your ideas for expansion are quite novel, Mr. Barnwell. Your workers should consider themselves fortunate to have such a benevolent employer. "

"Treat your workers well and they'll be yours for a lifetime," Uncle Bob said cheerfully. "That has always been the Barnwell way."

"One that has obviously worked. And now there's a question I would like to pose to you and Mrs. Barnwell."

"Of course, Mr. Russell," Aunt Laura said. He had specifically asked them not to use his title at the first of the evening.

He smiled again. "I should like permission to call on your niece while I'm in town. One seldom gets the chance to spend time with a young lady of her wit and sense of humor."

Her family exchanged glances and Aunt Laura asked, "Cassandra? What do you say?"

Her heart hammering against her stays, Cassandra said, "I should like that very much, Aunt Laura."

"Well then, the matter is settled," Uncle Bob said. "Please call anytime you like, Mr. Russell."

"Yes, do," Aunt Laura urged. "We're having an 'at home' this Sunday night. Why don't you join us?"

"I'd be delighted. Now, it's getting late and I still have a great many boxes of artifacts to unpack at the Museum tomorrow."

Brandon stood and bowed to his hosts. "Thank you for a delightful evening. I look forward to seeing you on Sunday."

"I'll walk you to the door," Cassandra said as she got to her feet.

In the foyer, she gave him his coat and hat. "Bravo, Brandon," she said softly.

He wiggled his eyebrows at her. "Do you think I made a good impression?"

"Your including Aunt Laura in asking permission to call on me won you full points," she replied. "She hates to be excluded in such things."

"Is she a suffragist like yourself?"

"Yes. She's organizing the rally I told you about."

Understanding dawned in his eyes. "Ah. The one where you will have yourself arrested and thereby ruin all future hopes for marriage."

"Yes," she said again. "Thank you for agreeing to help me."

She took a small folded piece of paper from her pocket and pressed it into his hand. He opened it and his eyes widened nearly to the size of saucers. "Good Lord. This is a check for fifteen hundred pounds."

"I told you that I have access to my own money. Consider it a first installment."

"And you are really prepared to go to these lengths to discover a man's true intent in courting you?" His tone was incredulous, as he pocketed her check.

Something like sorrow crowded around her heart but she gave him a brave smile. "There really is no other way," she said. "Marrying for anything less than true love is out of the question." She held out her hand in farewell. "Good evening, Brandon."

To her surprise, he lifted her hand to his mouth and kissed it. His lips' warmth flamed her skin and a heated flush swept over her body like a crashing wave.

Then he stepped back, bowed slightly and said, "Good night, Cassandra."

And then he was gone.

***

"Hold still," Cassandra instructed as she carefully glued the cotton to Brandon's eyebrows. "You can't appear as Father Christmas with blonde eyebrows and a white beard."

It was a curious feeling to touch him. She had never done more than shake his hand, or put her own hand around his arm. But to touch his face seemed terribly, terribly intimate and she forced herself to concentrate on her work, and not look into his eyes.

"I suppose not," he said. "How are you going to explain Father Christmas appearing early to the children?"

Laughing, Cassandra said, "I'm going to tell them that word has reached you that they have been particularly good, and you have come to thank them. As soon as the Christmas pantomime is finished, I'll lead you on stage and you'll pass out the gifts and candy. Then we'll have high tea."

This time she could not escape the mirth filled glance he shot her. "This is a Barnwell tradition for the children of their London employees?"

"We've done it for years," she said proudly. "But this is the first time we've ever had a visit from Father Christmas."

"Whose idea was that?"

Cassandra stepped back to admire her handiwork. "Mine, actually. But the Barnwell employee we had originally hired turned his ankle and we couldn't find anyone else at such a last minute." She took the false white beard and hat from the table and gave it to him. "I think you're ready."

He dutifully put them on and stood. It had taken two enormous pillows stuffed inside the rented red and white suit to make him appear fat enough for a true Father Christmas. If she had not helped prepare him, she never would guess that hidden underneath the Christmas finery was the strongly built figure of the man with whom she was now hopelessly in love.

It was beastly unfair, but she had no one but herself to blame. She had asked him, *hired* him to court her. It had all seemed so simple. Court her and convince any other possible suitors to keep their distance—which they had—while he pressed his own suit. Over the past few weeks, they had viewed picture exhibitions, gone to the theater and attended parties with Uncle Bob and Aunt Laura, and every day he had sent flowers. The gossip columns declaimed their doings on a near daily basis. Great Aunt Tilda was beside herself with joy.

She had not expected to fall in love.

"Penny for your thoughts, Cassandra."

His soft baritone intruded on her musings, and she shook herself from her reverie. "Just mentally going over the gift list," she offered. "Shall we go? Don't forget the toy bag."

She led him from the back room and towards the Assembly Hall of Barnwell's Fair Street factory. The excited shouts and laughter of children echoing from the hall showed the pantomime was already started.

They stopped at the stage door and she put a finger to her lips. "Not a sound now," she warned.

"Wouldn't dream of it," he said. "Are you nervous about tonight?"

"Not at all," she lied. "I'm looking forward to it."

Tonight his brother the Duke of Halstead was hosting a grand ball for his half-sister's approaching wedding. Great Aunt Tilda had fainted dead away when the heavily embossed invitation arrived at the house.

Aunt Laura and Uncle Bob had received one as well. Cassandra's ball gown had been delivered this morning and she could think of no better way to calm her nerves than by helping with this afternoon's pageant.

She opened the door and they silently climbed the stairs leading to the stage. The performers finished the final act to much clapping and exited on the opposite side of the stage. Cassandra took a deep breath and walked out. "Good afternoon, boys and girls!" she called.

"Good afternoon, Miss Barnwell," they shouted in return.

"I'm so glad you are here today, " she continued. "We have a lovely surprise for you. Because all of you have been very, *very* good, this year, someone wants to thank you. Father Christmas, are you there?"

"Ho! Ho! Ho!" a voice thundered from the wings. "Are there really good boys and girls here?" The massive figure lumbered on stage, waving to the shrieking children. "Ho! Ho! Ho!"

"Come here, Miss Barnwell, and help me pass out these gifts," Father Christmas said, as he set his bag down. "I'll just fetch that chair from the corner."

He slapped his belly and added, "I just hope it will hold my weight. Ho! Ho! Ho!"

The room rocked with laughter as he dragged the chair forward, sat and opened his bag. For the next hour, he presented tagged gifts, made jokes and patted heads. After the last child had skipped off the stage, he turned to Cassandra. "Well, Miss Barnwell," he boomed. "Is there anything else before the children have their tea?"

"No, Father Christmas, that's all."

He waggled his eyebrows at the children. "Don't you children think I have a very pretty assistant?"

"Yes!"

"What should I do to thank her?"

"Kiss her," shouted one boy.

"Kiss her! Kiss her!" The other children took up his cry.

"But we haven't any mistletoe," Cassandra shouted over their voices. "We can't have a kiss without mistletoe."

"I've got some." A little girl darted for the stage and mounted the steps. Plucking a sprig of the Christmas plant from her elf's hat, she gave it to the costumed-figure. "Here you are, Father Christmas. Now you can kiss Miss Barnwell."

"Thank you my dear," Father Christmas said, getting to his feet. "Well, Miss Barnwell, we can't disappoint them." He held the sprig over her head, gently pulled her into his arms and lowered his mouth to hers.

The world disappeared at the taste of his lips, sweet and soft, and the sound of her heart roaring in her ears all but drowned out the cheering of the children. His arms about her were warm and strong, and she knew if they were trapped forever beneath the dome of a snow-globe, she would be forever happy.

He pulled back, but kept his arms around for bit longer. She was grateful the beard hid his face but there was no mistaking the light shining in his eyes. He cleared his throat before he said loudly, "Happy Christmas, Miss Barnwell."

"And to you, Father Christmas." Blinking back her tears, Cassandra stepped out of his arms and waved to the children. "Who's ready for tea?"

***

By all the gods, Cassandra Barnwell was beautiful. Brandon stared at the woman approaching him from across the ballroom of Halstead House. Only a woman of Cassandra's coloring could wear a bronze and flame colored gown and get away with it. It made the other women's attire seem insipid, and put them all in the shade. Brandon imagined her hair billowing around her bare shoulders like a russet cloud, and his groin tightened. He really should have not kissed her this afternoon. The taste of her had stamped itself on his mouth, lingering like a promise of things to come.

But it was a promise that could never be fulfilled. Theirs was a business transaction, no more, no less, each getting what they wanted.

Or would they?

She reached him and offered a smile. "Good evening, Lord Brandon," she said formally.

"Good evening, Miss Barnwell. I'm glad that your family was able to come as well."

"Yes," she said without turning around. "Thank you for including them."

"Not at all. I believe the dancing is about to start. Shall we add to the speculation of our own impending engagement by waltzing?"

A shadow flickered in her eyes, but her smile remained. "Of course," she said gaily. "I do believe our scheme has been most successful."

Music began from the gallery overhead, and Brandon offered her his arm. Once in the ballroom he swept her out onto the floor and tried to ignore the knowing glances and nods as he wove her between the other dancers. As far as London was concerned, they were a nearly engaged couple.

If only it were true. But Cassandra Barnwell would never consider him as a matrimonial prospect. He had taken her money to play out this charade. Telling her he had fallen head over heels in love with her would only gain him a laugh. He could not of course, expect her to believe it.

Or would she?

The dance ended, and duty obligated him to dance with others. It wasn't until after the buffet supper, that he had the chance to speak with her again. It was one thing to be seen with her in the company of her family in public, quite another to flout convention by wooing her openly at a ball for his sister.

Because underneath Miss Barnwell's unconventional philosophies, Brandon suspected there beat the heart of a true romantic.

And by Heaven, he was going to find out one way or the other.

He found her talking to a dowager and politely asked for a moment of her time. The older woman smirked and stepped away. Cassandra looked up at him, her dark eyes full of question. "Brandon?"

"Join me on the balcony?"

"Let me fetch my shawl."

She returned in moments, the lacy garment draped around her shoulders. Outside the November air was strangely mild and they were alone. Moonshine covered the balcony with a day-like radiance, and in the soft light, Cassandra's face shone with something like expectation.

"So," she said.

"So." Brandon drew a long, slow breath before saying, "Cassandra–"

"Well, damn all, if I'm not a winner." Reeking of brandy, Freddie Vandergild staggered out of the shadows and gave them a lopsided grin. "And if I haven't found you at the very moment of proposing. You'll be glad to know Russell, old man, your share of the winnings from the bet will be at least five hundred pounds. That should keep you supplied for a long time, don'cha think?"

"Go to hell, Vandergild," Brandon ground out.

"Thas not very sporting of you," Freddie protested. "After all, a bet's a bet, and you didn't exactly say no. Old Bertie's gonna be most put out knowing he's lost. Course, it's not as if you need more money. Freckles here can give you all you need. That is if you can actually stand to marry her."

Cassandra's face paled. "You bet with others on whether you could convince me to marry you?"

"It's not like that," Brandon protested. "I told them–"

"And what better way to get more money for your work than to agree to my proposal," she continued flatly. "How very convenient."

"*She* proposed to *you*?" Freddie gasped. "Damn, she is a bluestocking, ain't she?"

85

"Shut up, Freddie. Cassandra—"

But she had backed away with a surprising speed and fled back inside the ballroom. Brandon grabbed his betrayer by the collar and dragged him to the wall.

"I hope you like thorns," he snarled, heaving Vandergild over the side into his sister-in-law's prize winning rose bushes twenty feet below. Vandergild's yelp as he landed among the thorns gave Brandon only a thimble of satisfaction when what he really wanted to do was break all four of Vandergild's limbs, one by one.

But this was his sister's night and he would not spoil it. He would finish his business with Freddie Vandergild and the entire membership of the Four In Hand Club later.

Right now he had to find Cassandra.

***

"She's not here, sir." The housemaid who had opened the door to Brandon wrinkled her forehead in thought. "Not sure where she's gone. Out early, even for her."

"Perhaps she went to the Barnwells?"

"She would have told Mrs. Mason that, sir," the maid said. " But she did look a bit pale. Perhaps she went walking in Hyde Park. She sometimes does that if she has a lot on her mind."

"Thank you," Brandon said, giving her his card. "If she comes home, please tell her I need to see her immediately."

If Elizabeth had not gone into labor in the middle of the ball, trapping him for hours until he knew the outcome, Brandon might have escaped Halstead House and found Cassandra by now. Explain he had no part in that damn stupid bet and give back her check. Report he had telegrammed Cairo with news the dig was indefinitely cancelled. Tell her his new twin nephews had arrived and he was off the dynastic hook.

Tell her he loved her.

How had it happened? *When* had it happened? He racked his brain for the moment but memory failed him. He only hoped he was not too late. Returning to the waiting cab, he directed it to Hyde Park and minutes later it was approaching the entrance. Hordes of people pushed and jostled one another as they fled out of it, their voices raised in panicked terror

Brandon kicked open the door and jumped out. Grabbing a passing man, he shouted, "What the hell is going on?"

"Riot," the man gasped, pulling free. "Some damn woman–". He ran away, clutching his bowler.

Cassandra! Please God, no. Brandon shoved his way through the escaping crowd and plunged into the madness filling Hyde Park.

"We'll have a demonstration after New Year's I'll be arrested for disturbing the peace." Cassandra's voice echoed in his head. Damn it, couldn't she have waited?

He spotted a crying woman talking to a uniformed bobby, and Brandon hurried forward. "Officer can you tell me what's happened?"

"Some woman favoring trade unions went and started a riot," the officer barked. "This here lady has lost her child in the ruckus."

A trade union activist. Brandon heaved an inner sigh of relief. *Not Cassandra after all. She'd never do anything that might harm a child.*

"He's only four," the woman wailed. She grabbed at the officer. "You gotta help me find my boy!"

"Lady, I've got a dozen missing people already–"

Brandon held out his hand "Come with me, madam. I'll help you find him."

Still sobbing, the woman put her hand around his arm and together they began their search. People continued to stumble past but it looked as if most of the crowd had made good their escape. Frantically Brandon scanned the opening space before them. How hard could it be to find Cassandra, with that glorious hair of hers, especially if she and the boy were together?

"Peter!" his companion screamed and dashed in the direction of a large oak tree. Brandon spied the duo seated under it and followed her.

Cassandra was holding a small boy in her arms. They were chatting as if neither had a care in the world, though her squashed hat and unbound hair showed things might have been lively a bit earlier.

"Hello, Mama!" the little boy called.

"You see, Peter? I told you she would find us if we just sat here and waited," Cassandra said.

Peter's mother's only answer was a heart-wrenching wail as she scooped up her son and carried him away. Cassandra waved and called, "Goodbye, Peter!"

Then as if she had just noticed him, she frowned and looked up. "How can I help you, Lord Brandon?"

"You can take back your check for starters," he said, helping her to her feet. "I don't need it anymore."

"Find another backer?" Her sarcastic tone lashed him "Someone prettier and more desperate than me?"

"Whether you believe it or not, Cassandra, I had no part in those bets." Brandon took her check from his pocket and stuck it among the flowers of her hat "The Russells never bet unless it's a sure thing. And even if I had agreed, how could I be sure you'd say yes? I had only met you that morning. I'm not *that* charming."

Hope replaced the anger in her face. "You didn't place a bet?"

"Cross my heart ." He traced his fingers over his chest. "Of course now that my brother's Duchess has presented him with twin sons early this morning, he's more than ready to back my future expeditions. But I've no plans on returning to Egypt anytime soon."

"You don't?"

"Not unless you'll come with me as my wife." He sank to his knees and took her hands in his. "Think of the fun we'll have. Camel races, playing in the world's biggest sand box—"

She giggled. "You heard about that, did you?"

"Yes. Somehow I don't think a Razzle-Dazzle girl would like the desert. The sun might give her freckles."

"I have freckles," she said proudly.

"Which is why I adore you and why you'll make the perfect wife for an archeologist." Brandon kissed her hands. "Other than the fact I love you madly and will probably die before morning if you don't say 'yes' to my proposal."

"You're as bad as Great Aunt Tilda," she scolded, getting up and pulling him to his feet. "I suppose I must save your life and marry you. But only because I love you madly and would probably have died before morning if you hadn't proposed."

He pulled her into his arms and kissed her far more thoroughly than he had the day before. "Then you can withdraw *your* original proposal, my love," he murmured, as he feasted on her lips. "My love is yours for the taking."

"A Christmas engagement," she sighed. "Great Aunt Tilda will be so pleased."

He raised his head, linked his arm through hers and began to walk them back through the park. "Shall we go tell her?"

Her smile banished any of his remaining fears. "Only if we stop to buy a new bottle of Crayfield's smelling salts first. I think she's going to need them."

The Comet That
Came for Christmas

Chapter One-❧

"You've invited *who* to spend the Christmas holidays with us?" Mary Hawthorne's usually pleasant alto voice soared an octave.

"Now, now, my dear," James Hawthorne soothed. "It's not exactly the Christmas holidays. Cyrus Higginbotham is coming tomorrow to spend a few days here to inspect Tyler as a possible location for his next Haley's Emporium. It could be a gold mine for Tyler! Think of the jobs it would create!"

"But Cyrus Higginbotham is a millionaire," Mary protested, her voice returning to its normal range. "We can't possibly accommodate him."

"Of course we can," James coaxed. "He'll only be here for three days at the most. Besides, we have the largest house in town and the best staff. The children

93

won't arrive until the day before Christmas Eve and you of course are the town's best hostess and cook."

His wife of nearly thirty years smiled at his praise. "Do you really think Mr. Higginbotham might open a Haley's Emporium here in Tyler?"

"I do," James said, excitement thrumming in his chest. "I've met him many times over the years on buying trips to New York and corresponded with him so regularly that he invited me to call him by his Christian name. *And* he has hinted he might make me General Manager if he does decide to open a store here."

"And with your experience, you are of course, the logical choice." Mary tweaked his collar with a wife's loving gesture. "Very well, my dear. We shall open our home to Cyrus Higginbotham, millionaire and entrepreneur. Will he be traveling alone?"

"I imagine he'll bring a personal assistant or secretary and a valet," James said. "I'll telegraph him before I go to the store. Thank goodness we had all those children and have enough empty rooms to accommodate him and his party, eh?"

He winked at her, and Mary blushed. "Really, James," she scolded. "The things you say!"

Laughing, James kissed her cheek. "I'm off to town then," he said. "Has Victoria already gone?"

"Our only daughter left early," Mary told him. "She's holding a special rehearsal at the school for the Christmas pageant before the day starts."

"I'll see you this evening then, my love." After kissing her again, James left the parlor. A minute later the front door clicked behind him.

Mary proudly looked around the large room with its comfortable chairs and sofas and piano. Theirs had been one of the first houses in Tyler to install electricity and have the most modern plumbing. And all modesty aside, Mary was a good cook, even though she had a kitchen staff.

"How does one entertain a millionaire?" she wondered aloud. "Will Mr. Higginbotham want to join us in such simple pleasures as our hunt for the perfect Christmas tree and reading of *A Christmas Carol* and. . . Good heavens!" Mary slapped a hand over her mouth. "What in the world does one feed a millionaire?"

***

December 20

It can't be. Not Tyler, Tennessee. Jackson "Jake" Dillon, stared at the rapidly approaching sign from the window seat of the train. Images long buried, first of a laughing girl with golden curls and merry green eyes, and then of the same girl weeping, flooded his memory.

Four years is a long time. She's probably married with children by now. Probably doesn't even live here anymore.

But you would think a man with a Harvard education would insist his employer tell him where they were going instead of letting him keep it a secret.

"Jackson! Have you fallen into a trance?"

The raucous voice of his employer sent the memories shuttling back into place. "No, Mr. Higginbotham," Jake said, forcing his thoughts to the day at hand. "Just looking at the area."

"I've heard tell it's a pretty little place," Cyrus Higginbotham tweaked his luxurious mustache. "Of course, I've only been to Nashville. May open a store there too."

"Is there a reason you chose Tyler instead of Nashville, sir?" Jake asked politely. *At least if we were visiting Nashville, I wouldn't run the risk of seeing Victoria Hawthorne again.*

"Heard Knoxville is a growing city." Higginbotham beamed at him. "Thought with Tyler being just fifteen miles away it would afford the folks here a better opportunity to do their shopping closer to home, don't you know. And get Knoxville folk to come here to shop. Boost Tyler's economy and create jobs, don't you know."

"Yes sir." Jake contained his yawn at Higginbotham's trademark phrase. The man had kept him up until past two in the morning, watching a shower of stars, convinced that Haley's comet, his personal talisman, would appear as a sign of the success of his new adventure in Tyler, Tennessee. "Comet's are like magic," he'd said, "making wishes come true."

Jake directed his gaze back out the window and listened to his late father's voice shout back at him from the grave.

Marry a girl from a hick town in Tennessee whose father is in trade? Have you lost your mind? Do you want to give your mother a nervous breakdown?

The train's braking pulled Jake out of the past. He watched the ever-silent Alfred, Higginbotham's valet seated across the aisle, stand and begin unloading the smaller of their employer's many bags from the overhead compartment. Jake did the same with his own, and waited for Higginbotham to put on his coat, hat, and scarf, step into the aisle and make his way briskly down the aisle.

"Are we staying at a hotel?" Jake asked, trying to keep up. Despite being almost fifty, Cyrus Higginbotham was broad shouldered and fit, often leaving others behind with his brisk stride.

"No room at the inns," Higginbotham called cheerfully. "Appropriate for Christmas time, isn't it? Don't think we'll have a white Christmas this far South. We're going to stay with the man who runs the town's largest department store. He keeps a good selection of Haley's stock there. Met him at a buyer's meeting years ago, and he's an excellent businessman. Says his wife is an incredible cook. You like to eat, don't you, Alfred?"

"Yes sir." Even at the suggestion of a good meal, Alfred's permanently dour expression did not waiver.

They followed Higginbotham out of his private car and stepped down onto the platform. A tall, well-built man in a dark blue overcoat and bowler hat, stood just under the awning leading to the station's interior. Higginbotham waved in greeting and shouted, "Hello, James!"

"Hello, Cyrus!" The man closed the distance between them in a few long strides, his hand outstretched. "Welcome to Tyler, Tennessee."

The men shook hands and Cyrus gestured over his shoulder. "This is my assistant, Jackson Dillon, and Alfred Bailey, my valet. Jackson, this is our host, James

Hawthorne."

Hawthorne? Oh my God. Good manners required a different response instead of Jake's silent petition to the Deity. "I'm very pleased to meet you, Mr. Hawthorne," he said, offering his hand. Hawthorne took it and gave it a hearty shake with a grin so like the blonde girl of recent memory that the old pain started in Jake's chest.

"My family and I are pleased to welcome you to our home," Hawthorne told him. "I've hired a wagon to bring the luggage to the house. My carriage is waiting if you'll just follow me."

"Excellent!" Higginbotham declared. "Can't wait to meet your wife and family, don't you know. Alfred, be a good fellow and see to the rest of the luggage."

The two older men headed toward the station and Jake looked at the powerfully built Alfred. "Do you need help?"

The valet shook his head. "Go on." He cast a baleful glance around the platform and added, "Do you think Himself could have dragged us any further from civilization?" His heavy New York accent suggested anywhere but that great metropolis was a barren wasteland.

"Look at it this way," Jake told him. "This far south, the chances of a snowstorm trapping us here are a million to one." It was snowing when they left Manhattan.

"Thank the Lord for that," Alfred groused. "I best be seeing to the bags. You there, porter! Can you help me, please?"

Jake left him to the business of the luggage and prayed that a certain young blonde woman who shared names with the last queen of England, would be anywhere but here in Tyler, Tennessee.

Chapter Two-🐚

Victoria Hawthorne locked her classroom door, eager to get home. More lively than usual because of the approaching holidays, her class of fifth graders had demanded every ounce of her patience these last few days before the school holidays. A long soak in the claw-foot tub in her bathroom with an extra scoop of rose-scented bath beads to perfume the water would be just the thing to refresh her.

Standing on the school's porch, she glanced down the street for Henry, the family's coachman and all around servant. Normally Victoria would have walked home, but a series of sneezes at the breakfast table this morning had convinced her mother—usually not given to "frets" about such things—that a cold was approaching and insisted Henry drive Victoria to and from school.

"'lo, Miss Vicki!" Henry's cheerful voice called, and she spied the little barrel-chested man driving the two-seater with D'Arcy, their black gelding leading the way. She hurried down the steps and climbed aboard when

Henry pulled D'Arcy to a stop. Watson, the family's cocker spaniel, wagged his tail in greeting.

"Have our guests arrived, Henry?" she asked as they moved forward again. A breeze fluttered the fringes of the canopy above them, and Vicki clutched her coat. Cold weather had finally arrived. Even in December, temperatures in Tyler often remained higher than other places.

"Yes, Miss Vicki. They arrived 'bout an hour ago." Henry turned D'Arcy around and headed back down the street. "And your mama's had Minnie cooking as if the President of these United States himself was coming to dinner."

At his easy-going observations, Vicki gave the gray-haired man a fond glance. She couldn't remember a time when Henry wasn't with her family. He and his wife Minnie, the family cook, were the only ones who still called her 'Vicki.' "What are our visitors like?"

"Mr. Higginbotham seems like a nice enough fella for a millionaire. Talks loud, but makes sense. The other—his valet and him that's his secretary or some such—hard to say. But—" the familiar twinkle started in Henry's eyes. "The secretary's not a bad looking chap. Maybe you could get a beau out of all this excitement about the new store in town, if it does open."

"Hush," Victoria commanded. She had sworn off beaus or any other romantic nonsense after her last year at Radcliffe. A broken heart was not exactly the kind of graduation present a young woman wanted or needed. Especially after being told her family wasn't good enough.

"Did you see any special stars or comets last night, Miss Vicki?" Like her, Henry was a devoted sky- watcher and they often spent evenings on the landing outside the library, her telescope trained on the sky, scanning it for celestial activity.

"No," Vicki sighed. "This is the year for Haley's Comet to be visible, but I don't think we've spotted even a trace of it, do you?"

"No, but maybe we'll get lucky, seeing as how it's almost Christmas. Maybe that's what the wise men saw."

"Maybe," Vicki agreed. "It would be nice to make a Christmas wish on Haley's Comet, wouldn't it?"

"It sure would," Henry agreed as they turned towards home. Lights flickered in the windows from the houses lining the streets, and Henry guided them towards the back of the Hawthorne home and the stable. They stopped, and Victoria climbed down. She came forward to stroke D'Arcy's velvety nose, and he gently butted her hand with his head.

"You rascal," she chuckled, taking the napkin wrapped apple slices she had saved from her coat pocket. "You never forget do you?" Giving apples to teachers was a school tradition in Tyler, and one firmly set in D'Arcy's mind.

The horse nodded as his mouth quickly took the apple from her hand and after another pat to his head,

Victoria headed toward the back porch off the kitchen. Inside, Minnie waved in greeting with one hand, and kept stirring the contents of the pot simmering on the stove, with the other. Watson headed for his basket and a nap.

"Your ma says you're to go straight to the parlor, Miss Vicki," she said. "I just sent in tea."

"Thanks, Minnie," Victoria called, unbuttoning her coat. In the hallway, she gave it and her scarf to Liz, their housemaid and continued on to the parlor, smoothing her hair. Obviously her bath would have to wait.

"–and of course, I would have dearly loved for one of my sons to follow me into the business but young people will have their own ideas and--ah, here's Victoria." Her father's words stopped as she entered, and her gaze went immediately to the tall dark-haired man standing before the fireplace, cup in hand.

Oh my goodness. Make that two scoops of bath beads. No, three. Victoria's heart began thumping at a rate more suited for making a mad dash from the room and up the stairs, which was of course, out of the question. What was Jackson Dillon doing in her home?

"Hello, my dear." Papa came to her side and kissed her cheek. "Come meet our guests." His hand under her elbow hardly gave her any choice as he guided her to the fireplace. A silver-haired man rose from the loveseat. across from her mother. Jackson Dillon remained motionless, but his eyes flickered in an uneasy dance, suggesting this meeting was not his idea either.

"Cyrus Higginbotham, allow me to present my daughter, Victoria," James introduced. "Victoria, this is Cyrus Higginbotham, founder of Haley's Emporium and our guest for the next several days. The gentleman standing over is his assistant and secretary, Jackson Dillon."

"Delighted to meet you, Miss Hawthorne." Mister Higginbotham bowed. "If I'd known there were such pretty young women in Tyler, I would have visited long before now." He chuckled at his own joke and her parents did the same.

"Welcome to our home," Victoria answered, folding her trembling hands together. Then silently apologizing for the lie, she added, "It's nice to see you again, Mr. Dillon."

"The pleasure is all mine, Miss Hawthorne." So said his lips, but a similar lie shone in his cobalt-hued eyes.

"You know each other?" Mama asked from the loveseat next to the teacart.

"Yes, Mama. Mr Dillon and I belonged to the same debating society my last year at Radcliffe," Victoria said, proud her voice didn't wobble. "He's very good with words and the turn of phrases." *Just like the words you used to capture my heart and then break it, you good-looking rat. And how incredibly unfair you're still just as good-looking.*

"Well then, I'm glad I brought you along, Jackson," Mr. Higginbotham said, rubbing his hands together. "Nothing like old friends meeting again, eh?"

"Yes, indeed." Victoria turned and went to sit beside her mother, returning her gaze to Jake's face. How dare he come here? She'd bet that new hat in the front window of Stanhope's Millinery shop he hadn't forgotten she grew up in Tyler, Tennessee. He used to tease her about the alliteration.

Might we one day have tea for two in Tyler, Tennessee?

With tasty toast and 'taters?

Hush, or I'll sing for you. Then you'll never survive college to attend Harvard Law.

She accepted a cup of tea from her mother. "Will you be in Tyler for long, Mister Higginbotham?"

"Only for a few days," he said, seating himself again. "Maybe three. We don't want to invade your home too much." He picked up his plate from a nearby table, chose a scone and bit into it. "Delicious," he pronounced. "Jackson, you've not eaten anything. Sit and try one of the sandwiches."

"Yes sir." Jake reluctantly joined his host. The loveseat was directly across from the one occupied by Victoria and her mother. Calling her Vicki as he once had somehow didn't seem right.

"How is your family, Mr. Dillon?" she asked, her tone as cool as a Long Island autumn breeze. "Are your parents well?"

Her question scraped along his skin like steel wool. "I'm sorry to say they have both passed away, Miss Hawthorne. Three and a half years ago, to be exact. Only my sister and I remain."

Shock chased the ever-present rosiness from her cheeks. "I beg your pardon, Mr. Dillon," she said softly. "I had no idea of your loss. Please forgive me."

"Thank you."

"I've never been to Manhattan," Mrs. Hawthorne said quickly with the skill of a battlefield strategist. "Won't you please describe it for me, Mr. Higginbotham?"

Whether he recognized his hostess' gambit or not, Cyrus Higginbotham plunged into a description of the area around his office, not far from Central Park, giving Jake the chance to remain silent and watch Victoria without appearing to be staring at her. Her lush figure filling out her ivory shirtwaist and blue narrow skirt was just as he remembered. Frail, delicate women had never appealed to Jake. Victoria had been equal to any suggestion he offered to row, ride or ice-skate, leaving all the other girls he knew in the shade.

He had never met anyone quite like Victoria Hawthorne.

"And the best thing about autumn in New York are the chestnut vendors," Cyrus sighed, finishing his description. "There are nothing like roasted chestnuts."

"Which is why our cook has prepared a chestnut stuffing for dinner tonight," Mrs. Hawthorne said shyly. "James recalled it as one of your favorites. Do you like chestnuts, Mr. Dillon?

Chestnuts. Another memory pierced its way through Jake's invisible armor as he remembered taste of Victoria's lips filled his mouth. "Yes to both, ma'am," he said, draining his cup. *Would it were something stronger than Earl Gray.*

Before he could ask for more, Victoria rose and crossed the carpet to take it from him. Her long, slender fingers brushed his, sending a blast of heat jolting up his arm. Her green eyes sparkled with the energy he recalled during their debate against a co-ed team from Yale and Vassar. He had often thought if one could harness her passionate energy, the world would have a new source of power. Victoria's arguments had helped carry the day, and his heart quickened as he recalled the impromptu kiss they shared under a chestnut tree as he walked her to her dormitory at Radcliffe after the train ride back to Boston.

She paused, deliberately keeping her fingertips on his, pinning him to his seat with her gaze before turning to carry the cup back for his refill. Her return visit to him and back to rejoin her mother was far quicker.

"Well, as soon as Jake has finished his tea, I'd like to freshen up before that fine meal you've promised us," Higginbotham said. "Are you done, Jake?"

"Yes sir." Determined not to let her think she had won, Jake drank the rest of the Earl Gray, rose and carried the cup to his host's daughter. He held it out, forcing her to touch his hand again. "Thank you, Miss Hawthorne," he said, mimicking her gesture of fingertip to fingertip, and he recognized the minute movement of her teeth catching the edge of her lips between them. He had unsettled her. Good.

"Then we'll see you gentlemen here at six-thirty for before dinner sherry," Mrs. Hawthorne announced as the men headed for the door. Jake's last glimpse of Victoria as he stepped into the hall was of her sitting, head slightly bowed, staring into his cup. Today was only Tuesday. It was going to be a long three days.

Chapter Three-🐚

December 22

"And so, since he was born in the same year Haley's Comet last appeared, Grandpappy decided he would name his first store after that event," Mr. Higginbotham explained over breakfast. "He always said, 'Hard work, honesty and thrift will take you far in business, but it doesn't hurt to have a little heavenly help. Like I told Jackson, comets bring good luck.'"

Victoria's parents laughed, and she managed a smile at the tycoon's story. Jake sat in silence, sipping his coffee. Obviously he had heard the story more than once.

"So, James." Mister Higginbotham reached for his fork. "What do we have planned for today?"

"I thought today we'd take the train out into the country," Papa said. "Once we're there, we can rent a cart and drive out to a Christmas tree farm."

"A Christmas tree farm?" Jake asked politely. "Do such things exist?"

"They're all over this part of Tennessee," Victoria said with forced sweetness. Being near him the past few days, even if only in the evenings, had been an agony. Thank goodness her job gave her the perfect excuse to leave the house. Having to pretend the only thing between them was they had once belonged to the same debating society instead of being a couple in love was the hardest thing Victoria had ever had to do.

But now school was out until the New Year, and Jake's smug formality didn't help one bit. Mama's whispered comments to Minnie about how beautiful his manners were didn't help either. Victoria made a mental note to pray very hard that the snow the Knoxville newspapers were predicting stay on the other side of the Cumberland Plateau, or at least until a certain too high-in-the instep personal assistant to a millionaire was long gone.

And she had been nice to him. Very nice. Because it looked more and more like Mr. Higginbotham would open a Haley's Emporium here in Tyler and make her father the General Manager. And she wouldn't take that chance away from Papa for the world.

Her fingers tightened around her fork as she asked, "Where do you get Christmas trees in New York City?"

"I never asked," he said coolly. "But Mr. Higgenbotham is considering selling them at Haley's next year, aren't you sir?"

"Yes indeed," Mr. Higgenbotham agreed, spearing another two sausages from the platter in the center of the table. "Maybe we can talk to the owner of the tree farm about that. Advertise 'pure Tennessee Christmas trees available at Haley's' in all the Manhattan newspapers, don't you know."

"Sounds good to me," Papa agreed. "Victoria, will you drive out with us?"

Victoria's brain frantically searched for an excuse. "I really need to grade some papers, Papa," she said. "Or at least begin to plan next semsester's lesson plans."

"Oh, please, Miss Victoria," Mr. Higginbotham pleaded. "This is my last full day in Tyler. Can't think of a better way to spend it than have a pretty girl show me the countryside. And we can talk about the kind of fashion you prefer. Southern ladies like pretty clothes, don't they?"

"Of course Victoria will go with you," Mama said firmly, giving Victoria the glance she recalled from childhood, the one that promised a quick and dangerous retribution if she did not agree to Mr. Higginbotham's request. "Won't you, Victoria?"

"Yes, Mama." The answer came to Victoria's lips automatically. "Isn't Henry supposed to drive you over to church this morning for your meeting about the Christmas rummage sale? How can he take us to the station if he's doing that?"

"Don't be silly, Victoria," Mama scolded. "It will take Henry—who is waiting for me in the kitchen—no more than fifteen minutes to get me to church and drive back here again. Please don't keep him waiting when he does. It was cold outside this morning when I took Watson for his walk."

So saying, she left the room, calling for Henry. Victoria watched her go, feeling Jake's eyes study her from over the rim of his coffee cup.

"Well then, we best get ready," Higginbotham announced. "Come along, Jake. Let's get our coats."

"Yes sir," and to Victoria's relief, her former love rose and followed his employer from the room.

Not five minutes later, bundled up against the cold, Victoria waited on the porch for Papa and their guests, watching for Henry and D'Arcy to return.

"It's only another day," she whispered. "Then Jake Dillon will ride out of my life again. No one will be the wiser, and that will be the end of that."

The floorboard creaked behind her, and the scent of bay rum enveloped her like an embrace. *His* scent. A scent he had always worn for luck during their debates, and later stamped itself on her clothing after a long kiss before parting for the night. Inhaling it now after so long, Victoria issued a silent command to her trembling knees not to fold beneath her as she turned. "Hello, Jake," she said softly.

"Hello, Vicki." He stepped closer and peered down at her. She had almost forgotten how tall he was.

But not how handsome. She would never, could never forget that.

"First time we're alone together," he commented. The graying light turned his eyes to nearly black. "You've been quite successful at avoiding me, Vicki."

"I've had things to do," she retorted, trying not to sound defensive. "Like teaching every day and help the children practice for the school Christmas pageant. Some of us do have to work for a living, you know."

"As a matter of fact, I do." He bit off the words and a smoldering anger surfaced in his eyes. "Perhaps it's a lesson I've had to learn late in life. But after one's family loses most of its money through bad investments, and then more of it by gambling, hoping to regain it and leaving one with very little left over, the only choice left is to work."

Lost their money? Victoria's fingers curled against her gloved hands. "I-I'm sorry," she said. "I didn't know that."

"My little lover of Sherlock Holmes hadn't deduced that I had to work?" A sneer entered his voice. "What did you think I was doing with Higginbotham?"

Embarrassment heated Victoria's face. "I don't know," she repeated stiffly.

He lifted her chin with his fingers. "So much for graduating magna cum laude from Radcliffe."

"Summa cum laude," she snapped. "But even that didn't make me good enough to marry into your family, did it?"

"Sorry it took so long, my dears." Higginbotham's breezy voice intruded on their talk. "But I simply had to have another quick sip of your mother's delicious coffee, Miss Hawthorne. Don't get coffee like that in Manhattan. So, now we're going to go find that perfect Christmas tree and–AAAARRRGGGGHHH!"

A roar issued from Cyrus Higginbotham's throat as his feet hit a patch of ice on the first step, plummeting him the rest of the way down to the pavement just as Henry pulled up at the curb with D'Arcy.

"Cyrus!" Papa catapulted out of the door but took his time descending the steps to kneel by a writhing Mr. Higginbotham.

"Sir!" Jake darted after him, and Victoria followed, joining him on Mr. Higginbotham's other side.

"My ankle!" Higginbotham groaned. "My back! By thunder, it hurts!"

"Don't move," Jake advised. He looked at his host. "Do you think we can carry him inside?"

"I wouldn't advise it," Papa said. "If his back is hurt, we don't want to risk further injury."

"Papa's right," Victoria said. "Doctor Bailey's office is only minutes away. Henry can have him back here in no time."

Papa stood and shouted, "Henry! Go get Doctor Bailey right away. But be careful!"

Nodding, Henry slapped the reins against D'Arcy's back, and the horse galloped off.

"Victoria, my dear, go get a blanket from the closet," Papa said. "We need to keep him warm until Henry gets back."

"Yes, Papa." Victoria stood and stepped forward, only to lose her balance and fall forward. A pair of arms grabbed her from behind and a delicious warmth carried on a wave of bay rum enfolded her again as she leaned against Jake's chest.

"Be careful, Miss Hawthorne," he warned, turning her around and holding her in place. "We don't need two injured people in the household."

"Thank you," she said. Stepping carefully, she made her way up the steps to enter the house, grab a blanket from the parlor sofa and return to the men. A light snow had started, spreading a lacy blanket of flakes over Cyrus Higginbotham.

"C-confound it, it's c-cold," the millionaire said through chattering teeth. "D-didn't know it got this cold in T-T-Tennessee."

Victoria gently laid the blanket over him. "Did you notice those big foothills when you arrived?" she teased. "Those were the Smoky *Mountains*. Bears live up there. Are you sure you want to open one of your Emporiums here?"

"Victoria, hush," her father pleaded. "Ah, thank goodness. There's Henry with Doctor Bailey."

A quick examination of Higginbotham by Doctor Bailey provided the diagnosis of severely pulled back muscles and a badly sprained ankle. After loading Higginbotham onto the stretcher he had brought, Bailey and Jake carried him into the parlor and helped settle him onto the sofa.

"I don't think we should carry him upstairs," Bailey said after giving Higginbotham a small dose of laudanum. "We need to move him as little as possible."

"But we're going back to Manhattan tomorrow," Jake argued. "We have a board meeting on Monday morning." *And one more night in Victoria's home will have me howling at the Tennessee moon.*

"Perhaps you do, sir, but not him," Bailey said firmly. "Pulled back muscles are serious. Several days' bed rest, perhaps a week is what he needs to make a full recovery."

"A week? You mean spend Christmas here?" Disbelief slammed into Jake's brain. Christmas in the Gobi would be a better option.

"If you want him to recover, yes," Bailey repeated.

"You just tell me what I need to do to take care of him, Doctor, and I'll do it." Alfred had entered the room, followed by Victoria. Obviously she had gone upstairs to tell him of his employer's accident.

"Oh dear," Hawthorne sighed. "I don't know what Mary will say about all this."

"Excuse me, Mr. Hawthorne." Henry joined the group. Snowflakes clung to the front of his overcoat. "But you best know that more snow is on the way. A lor of it. Pastor Anderson told me so when I dropped off Mrs. Hawthorne this morning. They're calling for at least six inches by tomorrow."

Gritting his teeth, Jake looked at his employer. "Congratulations, sir. Looks like you're going to have a white Christmas after all."

Chapter Four-

Later that afternoon...

"I need to go into town and send some telegrams before I return to Manhattan."

Doctor Bailey had gone, and at least for now, Cyrus Higginbotham was snoring on the parlor sofa. Listening to Jake's declaration, Victoria watched him pace her father's office. She blinked back the unexpected tears pricking her eyes as she recalled trying to keep up with his long-legged stride during autumn hikes with their friends. He'd nicknamed her Crazy Legs while she learned to negotiate the winding trails. Now, it seemed like such a long time ago.

"You must do what you think best, but if what Henry says about the approaching bad weather is true, I wouldn't count on returning to Manhattan any time soon," Papa warned. "Ahh-ahh-choo!"

"Papa, are you catching cold?" Victoria took the handkerchief tucked inside her belt and gave it to him.

"Not at all my dear. Ahh-ahh-ahh-choo!" Her father buried his face in the cloth's delicate folds.

Jake stopped and shoved his hands into his pockets. "Mr. Higginbotham has *never* missed a board meeting. And since he can't travel, he'll need me there as his representative."

"Then let's hope for both your sakes, the trains will be running tomorrow. Ahh-ahh-choo!"

"Agreed," Jake said. "Can Henry take me to the telegraph office?"

"Mama had a list of things for him to do so he's out with D'Arcy," Victoria put in. "I'll hitch up Dickens and drive you to the telegraph office, Mr. Dillon. It's at the train station."

"But it's snowing, Victoria," her father protested. "I can take Mr. Dillon to send his telegrams."

"Papa, you've sneezed three times in two minutes," Victoria said. "Mama will have forty fits if you get sick from being out in the cold. Besides, I can drive in the snow as well as you can. You stay here in case she comes home early. Get your coat, Mr. Dillon."

She marched into the hall and took her coat and scarf from the closet. After putting them on, she made her way back through the kitchen and out to the barn, where she hitched old Dickens to the wagon, got in, and drove him into the yard. Jake Dillon, suitably attired for the weather, came down the back steps and waited for her to join him. Climbing up beside her, he said, "I can drive if you like."

Two bright patches of red appeared on her cheeks as she took a pair of gloves from her pocket and pulled them on. "I know how to drive."

"I know you do," Jake said, trying not to recall the lacy hat she wore in the spring when they, along with some friends, took the train into the country to rent pony carts and drive about. She was the prettiest woman there, and she had been with *him*. "A gentleman always drives when a lady is with him."

Something like a pout hovered around her lips. "Is that another silly New York Society rule? Besides, Dickens doesn't like strangers. If you try to drive him while I'm sitting here, he'll either bolt, or just stand there."

Her tone, not to mention the rapidly falling flakes, only added to Jake's aggravation. "Don't be perverse."

"See for yourself," she said, handing him the reins. "But don't say I didn't warn you."

"Get-up, Dickens," Jake commanded, flicking the reins against the horse's back. Dickens shot Jake a defiant stare before turning his head away, feet planted firmly in place.

"I said, get-up," Jake's voice rose as he slapped the reins again. Dickens remained where he was.

"Satisfied?" Victoria took the reins and called, "Take us to town, Dickens."

The little white horse trotted forward, and soon they were moving down the street at a surprising pace. Snow swirled around them, making tiny pinpricks of light in the surrounding overcast sky. Only one or two wagons passed them, and they rode on in silence.

"I'm sorry," Jake said at last.

"That's quite alright," she countered, keeping her eyes on the road.

"I mean, I'm sorry for everything," he amended. "I didn't mean to hurt you, Vicki. I never should have said you and your family weren't good enough. Your parents are fine people."

Her eyes flickered at him, then returned to focus on the road. "Really?"

He nodded. "My parents were obsessed with their position in Society and about having the 'right' kind of people as friends. And do you know what? When Father lost most of his money in bad investments and then nearly all the rest in gambling to try to regain it, those so-called 'friends' turned their backs on them. The shock killed both my parents, and I had to scramble to salvage what was left so my sister Eleanor could have some kind of security. My great-aunt Rosalind reluctantly took her in, but I was on my own."

She pulled on the reins, slowing Dickens from a brisk trot to a slow walk. "So that's why you're working for Cyrus Higginbotham," she said. "I'm sorry for what happened, Jake. I truly am. People need friends when something like that happens to them."

"I seem to remember you didn't care for the Society papers," Jake said, lightening his tone. "So you wouldn't have heard what happened."

"And *Tyler Today* probably wouldn't have reported it anyway." She looked at him and her sudden grin lit up her face and warmed his heart. "It's a small newspaper that comes out three times a week. And *Tyler Today* only reports the talk of Tyler town. Is that alliterative enough for you?"

They both laughed, and a wave of affection for her swept over Jake. How could he have ever agreed with his parents about her not being good enough?

Coward. The old accusation echoed his head. *You're a coward. If you'd really loved her, you would have stood up to your father.*

"So what have you been doing with yourself all these years?" he asked. "You said something about a job?"

"I teach fifth grade at one of the schools," she said. "I had to go to a teaching seminary for a year to qualify, even though I had a degree in English from Radcliffe."

"Do you enjoy teaching?"

Her face lit up with the enthusiasm he had never quite forgotten. "I love it. The children can be a challenge at times, but for the most part they behave and are eager to learn."

"And I'm sure you make learning fun," he said. "You always did have a zest for life, even for the simple things."

"Sometimes simple things are the best," she said.

"What could be more fun than driving through the country or ice skating on a frozen pond and coming back to warm up with hot cider?"

Her recitation of things they had done together brought a lump to Jake's throat and he coughed it away.

"Not much," he admitted. "Not much."

She halted Dickens in front of the train station. Jake jumped out, pulled down the wagon's steps and held out his hand. Her long, slender fingers wrapped around his palm, and as she descended the steps, he impulsively wrapped his hands around her waist and lowered her to the ground. Her hands slid up to his shoulders and her eyes widened, watching him and waiting.

"You forgot to wear a hat," she whispered, brushing the snowflakes from his hair. "You don't want to get sick, do you?"

"No." Jake's heart began to hammer with a rib-bruising force and he lowered his head to brush his lips against hers in a feathering sweep. He heard her sharp intake of breath and his arms slid down to her waist. "Victoria," he whispered. "I–"

A train whistle's shrill scream interrupted him. "We better get those telegrams sent," she said, stepping back and making her way to the station door.

Silently cursing the train's arrival, Jake followed her, the rumble of wheels pounding in his ears. Could things ever be made right between them?

He joined her at the telegraph counter and wrote out the needed messages. Handing them to the clerk, he asked, "What have you heard about the weather?"

The man grimaced. "A blizzard has already hit Virginia and is coming this way, not to mention the one coming over the plateau."

Anxiety speeded up Jake's heart. "Then you would advise against traveling?"

"Mister, I wouldn't travel with anyone right now but Santa Claus, and even he might have trouble getting through. The last train just got here, and only a fool would try to get in or out of Tyler with that snow coming."

"I see," Jake said. "Thank you."

"Oh dear," Victoria murmured. "I suppose that means my brothers and their wives won't be able to come for Christmas. Mama is going to be so disappointed."

"Mr Dillon! Yoo-hoo, Mr Dillon!"

They turned, and Jake's mouth fell open as the tall, buxom brunette in an oversized hat and white fur-collared coat rushed forward, arms outstretched. A slender woman, carrying a large carpetbag, staggered behind her.

"Miss Carson?" Jake gasped.

"Yes, it's me!" she chirped. "Surprise!"

"But what are you doing here?"

She clutched her gloved hands together. "The Manhattan papers said the weather here might be terrible! So I says to myself, Bertha, you can't miss a Christmas with your Cyrus! So me and Daisy--"she pointed at the woman who had stopped and put down the carpetbag--"caught the last train from Union Station for Tennessee, and here we are!"

She fluttered her eyelashes and gave Victoria a friendly smile. "Hello," she said. "Who are you?"

Shoulders shaking with what must be silent laughter, Victoria held out her hand, and said, "I'm Victoria Hawthorne, Miss Carson. Welcome to Tyler, Tennessee."

Chapter Five

He kissed you. Jake Dillon kissed you.

"Victoria, did you hear what I asked?"

Victoria blinked. "Sorry, Mama. I put Daisy in one of the empty bedrooms in the servants' quarters. She seemed awfully pleased to have a bathroom to herself."

"But where are we going to put *her?*" Her mother stared in dismay as a cooing Bertha Carson hovered around a now fully awake Cyrus Higginbotham, propped against a mountain of pillows on the parlor sofa. From the man's expression, he was obviously enjoying her attentions. Alfred waited in the corner, awaiting instructions.

"If the boys aren't going to be able to make it, we can put her in one of their rooms," James suggested. "Are you sure the station master said there would likely be no more trains arriving today, Victoria?"

"Yes, Papa." Victoria covered her mouth to stop the giggle hovering behind her lips. Cyrus Higginbotham looked as happy as a pig in a July mud pond. She shot a glance at Jake. The merriment sparkling in his eyes proved he shared her mirth.

Then the merriment vanished, and something else sparkled there. A something that sent a tingle racing over Victoria's skin. "And Miss Carson can help entertain Mr. Higginbotham during the holidays," she said aloud.

"Hey, listen." Bertha rose from her place on the sofa and came forward. "I know my coming is a surprise, but if my staying here is gonna be a problem, then I can stay at a hotel."

"I won't here of it," Papa said hastily. "We have plenty of room, don't we, Mary?"

"Mr Higginbotham wouldn't be happy if you weren't here to help take care of him," Mama said politely, but Victoria heard the resignation in her voice. Mama didn't like to be caught off guard.

Bertha gave them a glittering smile. "That's alright, then." She glanced around the room. "Don't you folks have a Christmas tree?"

"We were going to go find one until I fell down the steps," Cyrus grumbled. "Now I've gone and ruined that and everyone's holiday."

A chorus of denial filled the room. "I'll send Henry after one," Papa said when the noise died away. "I'd send Victoria with him, but she has a rehearsal this evening for tomorrow night's school Christmas pageant, don't you my dear?"

"Goodness," Victoria gasped. "I'd nearly forgotten that in all the excitement." *Being kissed by Jake Dillon again after all these years could do that to a girl.*

"Well, I think I better go see about dinner," Mama announced. "James, after we eat, perhaps Alfred can help Henry set up a bed for Mr. Higginbotham in the old sewing room. It's big enough and we can't let him sleep on the sofa while he's recuperating. He needs privacy while he's resting, and we'll need room in here for the tree. Could you do that for us, Alfred?"

"Yes ma'am."

"I hope you found your bedroom to your liking?"

"Yes ma'am," Alfred repeated. "And if I may so, I can't remember when I've tasted better cooking."

"Excuse me, Mrs. Hawthorne?" Liz hovered in the doorway. "Dr Bailey has sent over a wheelchair for Mr. Higginbotham. Shall I bring it in?"

"Yes, of course," Mama said. "How very thoughtful of Dr Bailey."

"I know everything I'd heard about Southern hospitality wasn't exaggerated," Higginbotham proclaimed. "Didn't I say that on the way down, Jake?"

"Yes sir, you did."

"Miss Carson, may I show you to your room?" Victoria asked.

"That would be nice," their newest guest agreed. "Cyrus honey, don't go anywhere."

Upstairs, Victoria opened the door next to her room. "We thought this might suit you."

"How pretty!" Bertha stepped inside and nodded in approval. "Blue and white are my favorite colors. Are you sure I'm not putting someone out?"

"Not at all," Victoria assured her.

"Good." Miss Carson took off her hat and tossed it on the bed before turning to face Victoria, chin raised. "Now, I want to get one thing straight with you, Miss Hawthorne. There ain't nothing improper between Cyrus and me. I may be a chorus girl, but I don't fool around with no one. Cyrus is the only man who didn't expect something from me after taking me to dinner or the theater, if you know what I mean. We've been courting for two years and he's never been nothing but a perfect gentleman. So you don't need to worry about anything happening between him and me while we're under your roof."

Victoria leaned against the doorframe at the young woman's long-winded declaration. "Why aren't you and Mr. Higginbotham married?" she asked.

Bertha shrugged and made a face. "He's got a bee in his bonnet about not getting married 'til he turns fifty." Then she smiled and added, "But that's on New Year's Day, so I'm hoping he'll...."

Her voice trailed up in expectation, and Victoria laughed. "Perhaps Dr. Bailey will let him travel back to Manhattan by then."

"I hope so. I'm sure Tennessee is real nice, but it sure ain't Manhattan, Miss Hawthorne."

"Victoria."

Her new friend smiled again. "Then call me Bertha. I never did believe in standing on ceremony. And boy, isn't that Jake Dillon easy on the eyes?"

Color flooded Victoria's face. "Yes," she admitted reluctantly. "He is."

"Victoria? Miss Carson?" Mama called from downstairs. "Dinner is ready."

"Come on, Vicki." Bertha came forward and linked their arms. "I'll bet if you play your cards right, you could get a proposal out of Jake Dillon by New Year's Day. I saw the way he was watching you. You've already got his goose cooked good and proper. Course you'd have to move to Manhattan. He's such a city boy, he'd never live anywhere else."

And I could never live anywhere else but Tyler. The hope stirring in Victoria's heart shrank back into its hiding place as she let Bertha lead her downstairs to the dining room.

December 23

"And so then, we went for a carriage ride through Central Park and the night sky was full of shooting stars! It was the most romantic, magical evening of my life and I knew right there, Cyrus was the only man for me!" Bertha sighed and dabbed her eyes with her breakfast napkin.

The other guests laughed softly at the blush covering Cyrus Higginbotham's face. "Go along with you," he said gruffly.

After dinner last night, Victoria had gone to the pagent's last rehearsal, leaving a much recovered Mr. Higgenbotham, her father and Jake deep in a disuccion of the new Haley's Emporium. When she returned, she found their guests and her parents playing whist in the parlor. For two native New Yorkers, Mr. Higginbotham and Bertha seemed to be settling in quite nicely. Jake had retired for the evening. Earlier, Bertha had proved quite handy with a needle–"us chorus girls have to keep our costumes in good repair,"–and helped Mama with her sewing, and kept Mama laughing with funny stories about the theatre.

Which was good, because being alone again with Jake was something she didn't think she could risk. Another one of those kisses would undo her.

Now, as Henry and Minnie cleared the table, Bertha asked, "What are you going to do about your Christmas tree, Mr. Hawthorne?"

"Well," Papa said slowly, exchanging glances with his wife, "Henry said there's a farmer selling them on the square. Perhaps we could start there."

"Can we go look at them?" Bertha pleaded. "I'm sure with all these muscled men, we can get Cyrus' chair into a wagon or cart– if you have one–so he can go with us. After all, he's had a full day's rest. Cyrus honey, don't that sound like fun?"

"My dear, it sounds splendid. And you're right. I'm feeling much better. James, are the streets clear enough?"

"As a matter of fact, they are," Papa said. "I suppose we can use that old flatbed wagon to go look at the trees."

"James, have you forgotten you have a vestry meeting at church this morning?" Mama asked. "And I must mend the tablecloth we'll use for Christmas dinner. Victoria and Mr. Dillon can drive them into town but they need to hurry. More snow is coming. I just hope it doesn't cancel tonight's Christmas pageant."

And so, half an hour later, after securing the wheelchair to the back of the flatbed wagon, and with some assistance from Alfred and Henry, Cyrus sat beside Bertha on the second passenger seat behind Jake and Victoria. Picking up the reins Victoria called, "Take us to town, Dickens."

As they drove into town, Victoria pointed out the different styles of the houses lining the street. Judging from the soft giggles and conversation behind her, she doubted that Higginbotham and Bertha were listening.

And she was quite aware of the man beside her. A warmth radiated from him, filling her with a calm she hadn't had since his arrival.

"I've never picked out a Christmas tree before," he said suddenly.

Victoria canted her head towards him. "Never?"

"No. My parents always had one sent in from the countryside."

Hearing the wistful regret in his voice, Victoria's heart gave a sympathetic twist. "Then we'll let you pick out the tree."

The look he gave sent an entirely different feeling surging through her. "Thank you. I'd like that."

They rode on in silence until they came to the town square and the tree-farmer. Victoria pulled Dickens to a stop, and Jake scrambled out to assist her down. His hands curved around her waist and his breath caught in his throat at the feel of her under his hands. He offered her his arm, and they stepped forward to move between the trees.

"How about that one?" She pointed.

"Too short."

"That one?"

"Too skinny."

She giggled. "So you want a tall, fat tree?"

"You do have high ceilings, Miss Victoria, and more than enough space. I think *that* one, over there." Jake strode over to stand beside a tall, thick fir tree and wrapped his hand around a branch. "This one should fit perfectly in the corner of your parlor."

"I think you're right," Victoria agreed. "Should we carry it back for the others to see?"

A smile lifted the corners of his mouth. "Somehow, I don't think they're going to notice it very much. Or us."

She turned her head and gazed at the couple in the wagon. "I think you're right." Looking up, she added, "And I also think we need to start back. That sky is looking more snow-filled by the second."

After arranging for the farmer to send the bill to Mr. Hawthorne's office, Jake shouldered the tree and headed back to the wagon with Victoria by his side. "Is that the way business is done here?"

"You mean the farmer trusting my father will pay him? For things like that, yes. But we use cash too, in case you're worried."

He shot her a glance but found only a smile on her face. "No swapping produce for services?" he teased.

Her eyes twinkled. "Sometimes we do that."

They loaded the tree behind Higginbotham's wheelchair and took their places in the wagon again. As Jake predicted, the other couple didn't even notice them. Victoria picked up the reins once more and they headed back to the Hawthorne house, just as the sky opened up and it began to snow. By the time they arrived, a blinding gust of white flakes swirled around them. A waiting Henry and Alfred hurried from the front porch and helped unload Cyrus and his chair. Bertha climbed down unaided and assisted the men with getting the millionaire into the house. Victoria drove Dickens back into the barn and unhitched him, while Jake unloaded the tree. Shouldering it again, he gave her a thoughtful look. "Thank you. This was fun."

"Simple things," Victoria said softly. "Remember how we enjoyed doing simple things?"

He nodded. "Vicki I--"

"Miss Vicki, your mother says for you and Mr. Dillon to come inside right now before you freeze to the ground!" Minnie called from the back porch. "The temperature's dropped four degress in the last hour!"

"We better go inside," Victoria whispered as she hurried into the yard.

And containing his sigh, Jake followed Victoria into the house.

Chapter Six-🍂

"Oh dear, there's hardly anyone here," Mary whispered. "The children will be so disappointed. So will Victoria."

The snow continued throughout the rest of the day, and by six o'clock, Tyler was nearly buried. A whistling wind rattled the windows, and only the tiniest flicker of light from the streetlamps pierced the swallowing darkness. Fewer than twenty people–most of them parents–sat in the school auditorium.

"Somehow I don't think Victoria will let that stop the show from going on," James said softly. "She's worked too hard."

"I think you're right, Mr. Hawthorne," Jake also whispered. "When she was preparing for a debate at school, Victoria prepared harder than any of us. She won't let something like a blizzard stop her or her pageant."

"That's right, Mr. Dillon," Bertha declared. "People won't let a little snow stop them from coming to see their kids perform. It's gonna be wonderful! Right, Cyrus honey?"

"You bet." The millionaire nodded in agreement.

And as if on cue, the doors opened and people bundled up in coats, hats and scarves, streamed into the auditorium, filling the seats, just as a burst of music began from an upright piano on the stage, and a horde of children filed out and mounted the bleachers in front.

"You see?" Bertha crowed. "The show must go on!"

A series of Christmas songs and skits followed, delighting the assembly. From the children's smiling faces and happy voices, they didn't care about the bad weather either.

And judging from the applause when the show ended, neither did their parents. Especially when two of the boys pulled Victoria from the wings, forcing her to take a bow with her charges.

But the howling wind speeded the exit of cast and audience from the school, sending them scurrying for the safety of their homes. Back at the Hawthorne's house,

Minnie passed around cups of hot chocolate and a plate of decorated sugar cookies.

"Here's to Tyler's best director!" James announced, raising his cup.

"Hear, hear!" the others called.

Victoria smiled. "Thank you," she said. "Pageants are fun, but I'm exhausted." She glanced at the decorated tree in the corner. "We did a good job on that this afternoon, didn't we? I'm glad we finally got it up."

"I thought you might be too tired to do it after the pageant," her mother said. "I think it's the prettiest tree we've ever had, thanks to our visitors."

"It has the Manhattan touch," Bertha said, and they all laughed.

"Too bad about the snowstorm," Henry said glumly. "Papers said Haley's Comet might have been visible tonight, but you can't see anything now."

"That's too bad," Victoria sighed. "I was hoping we'd at least have shooting stars to make Christmas wishes on."

And it would take something like Haley's Comet to wish on for Jake Dillon to stay in Tyler.

"Well, I think this is the most fun I've had at Christmas in years," Higginbotham announced. "I think I might want to spend every Christmas in Tyler from now on, don't you know. What do you say, Bertha, my dear?"

The chorus girl leaned over to kiss her beau on the cheek. "Whatever you say, Cyrus honey."

The happy pair brought a sting of tears to Victoria's eyes and she set her cup on the table. "If you'll excuse me, I'm going to say good-night."

Jake rose. "Congratulations on the pageant, Miss Hawthorne," he said. "Nicely done."

"Thank you, Mr. Dillon. I'll see you all tomorrow at breakfast."

And with that, Victoria hurried from the room.

***

"Vicki? Vicki, wake up."

"What?" Victoria blinked her way out of a sleep haze and sat up to see Jake Dillon standing on the landing outside her room in his dressing gown, the door to it slightly open.

"Put your robe on," he hissed. "And hurry."

He closed the door and Victoria shoved aside the bedclothes. Hurrying to grab the robe draped over the back of a chair, she shrugged into it and tied the sash before joining him. "Have you lost your mind?" she whispered. "If my parents find us--"

"Look." He pointed overhead.

"Oooh." She let out a long sigh as she raised her gaze from his face. "Oh, Jake."

A flurry of stars chased each other in gleeful abandon across the black landscape of the sky. "You were saying something about Christmas wishes?" Jake asked.

"Star light, star bright," Victoria chanted.

"But there are so many stars," Jake countered, stepping behind her to rest his chin on her head. "Which one should we wish on?"

Suddenly, above them, an enormous light streaked across the sky, adding its own particular brilliance to the night. They watched the majesty of it until it vanished from their sight. "*That* one," Victoria whispered. "Do you think that was Haley's Comet?"

"I think I'd rather call it Vicki's." Jake turned her about. "Vicki, I've been a complete ass. I should have asked you to marry me four years ago, but my parents–"

"Hush." Victoria laid a finger on his lips. "I understand. And you've had your sister to worry about."

"But if he'll allow it, I'm going to ask Cyrus to let me stay in Tyler and work in the new store. I'll take any job he offers, even if it's sweeping floors. Just say you'll give me another chance."

The hope shining in his eyes outdid the stars above them and she wrapped her arms around him. "Are you asking me to marry you?"

He laughed and pulling her closer, leaned down to brush his lips against hers. "I always said you were the smartest woman I knew."

"Even if it means tarrying in a tiny town like Tyler, Tennessee?"

"Alliteration again?"

She brushed a lock of hair away from his forehead. "Can you think of something better?"

"To paraphrase the Bible, whither thou stayest, I will stay," he whispered. "Or something like that."

Trying not to choke on her tears, Victoria said, "Well then, Mr. Dillon. Welcome home to Tyler, Tennessee."

And their kiss took away the need for more words.

***

The two men watched from the greenhouse directly across from Victoria's room a moment longer, then slipped back through the parlor's French doors.

"You deserve an award for your performance," James praised, once they were inside. "One would think you'd seriously hurt yourself. Where did you learn to do a fall like that?"

"Theatricals," Cyrus chuckled. "Hated to lie, don't you know, but since snow in Tennessee is sometimes rare, I thought I'd best create a situation where we couldn't leave. I'd have found a way to keep Jake here if he'd tried to get back to Manhattan. That boy has been pining for your daughter for years. Never would have known, if he hadn't got drunk one night this spring and spilled out his heart."

James laughed softly. "Took us long enough to put our plan together, didn't it?"

"Well, I had those other stores to open," Cyrus reminded him. "And dragging Jake all over the country watching me do it will help him when I name him co-manager of the new Haley's here in Tyler. Remind me to send the doctor a case of his favorite wine for helping in our little charade."

"Victoria can be as stubborn as an Army mule, never admitting when she's been hurt," James added, pouring them each a brandy. "It isn't like her to leave her diary lying open, much less in the parlor. I'd never have known about Jake if I hadn't seen his name on the page when I closed it. Well, 'the course of true love never did run smooth' to quote the Bard."

Cyrus chuckled again. "I think it's running smoothly enough now. After all, our lovebirds had help from the magic of the comet."

ABOUT THE AUTHOR

A life long Anglophile, Karen Hall loves 19th and early 20th century British history. She lives in East Tennessee with Buddy and Febe the wonder dogs. When not writing she loves music, cooking for friends and tries to keep the flowerbeds weeded.